Boys for a **The** Better World

GOOD GUYS
AGENCY

Brave like Jackie Robinson

For my wife, Cynthia, and all
of the people who don't realize
how truly brave they are.
—N. E.

**BUSHEL
& PECK
BOOKS**

Text copyright © 2022 by Nick Esposito.
Illustrations copyright © 2022 by Ricardo Tokumoto.

Published by Bushel & Peck Books, a family-run publishing house in Fresno, California, that
believes in uplifting children with the highest standards of art, music, literature, and ideas.
Find beautiful books for gifted young minds at www.bushelandpeckbooks.com.

Type set in LTC Kennerly Pro, Pilkius Romeus, and Impact Label
Some visual elements licensed from Shutterstock.com
Sources consulted: The Jackie Robinson Foundation (jackierobinson.org)

Bushel & Peck Books is dedicated to fighting illiteracy all over the world. For every book we
sell, we donate one to a child in need—book for book. To nominate a school or organization to
receive free books, please visit www.bushelandpeckbooks.com.

Boys for a **The** Better World
GOOD GUYS AGENCY
Brave like Jackie Robinson

Nick Esposito • **Illustrated by Ricardo Tokumoto**

Welcome back!

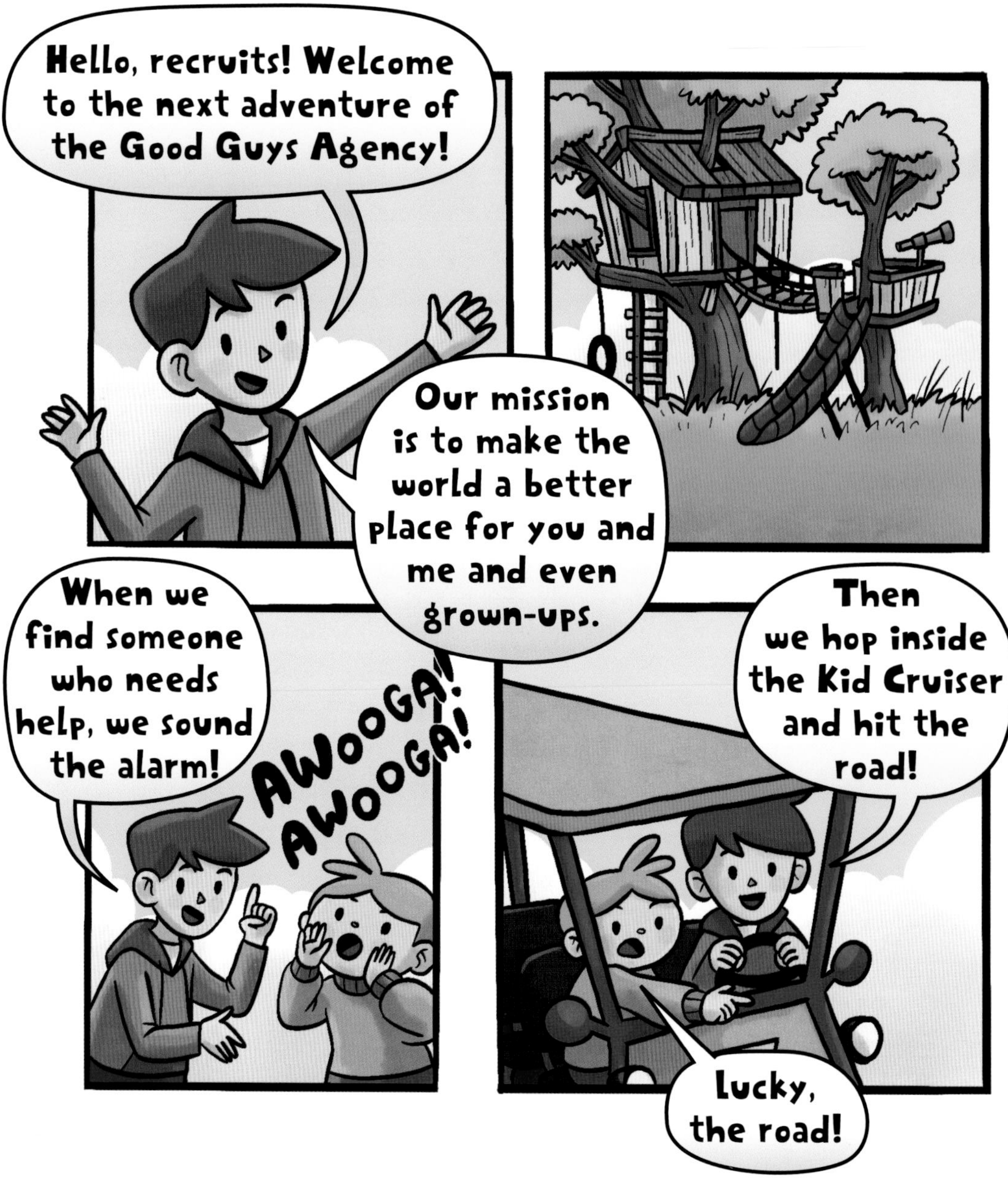
Hello, recruits! Welcome to the next adventure of the Good Guys Agency!
Our mission is to make the world a better place for you and me and even grown-ups.
When we find someone who needs help, we sound the alarm!
AWOOGA! AWOOGA!
Then we hop inside the Kid Cruiser and hit the road!
Lucky, the road!

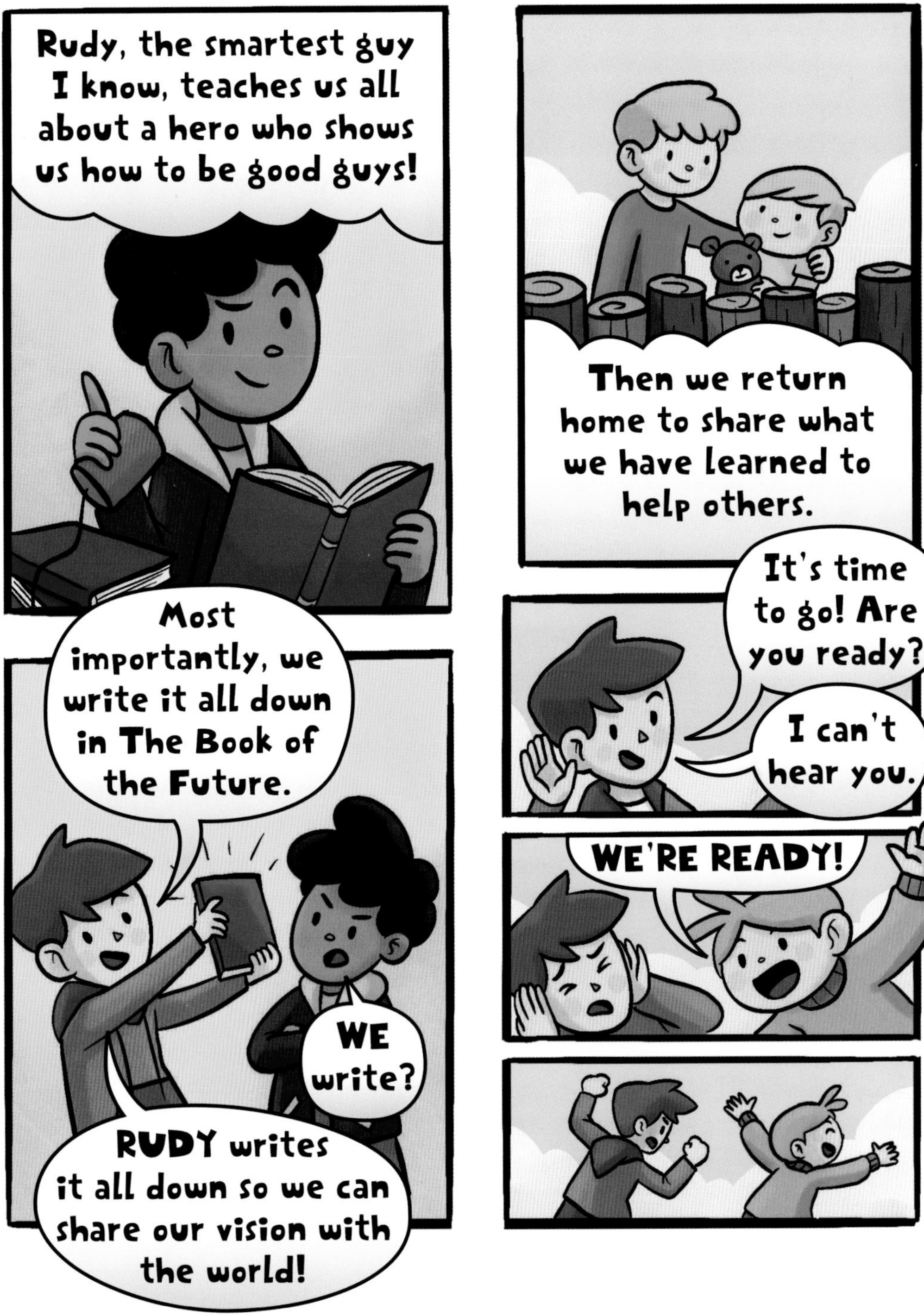
Rudy, the smartest guy I know, teaches us all about a hero who shows us how to be good guys!
Then we return home to share what we have learned to help others.
Most importantly, we write it all down in The Book of the Future.
WE write?
RUDY writes it all down so we can share our vision with the world!
It's time to go! Are you ready?
I can't hear you.
WE'RE READY!

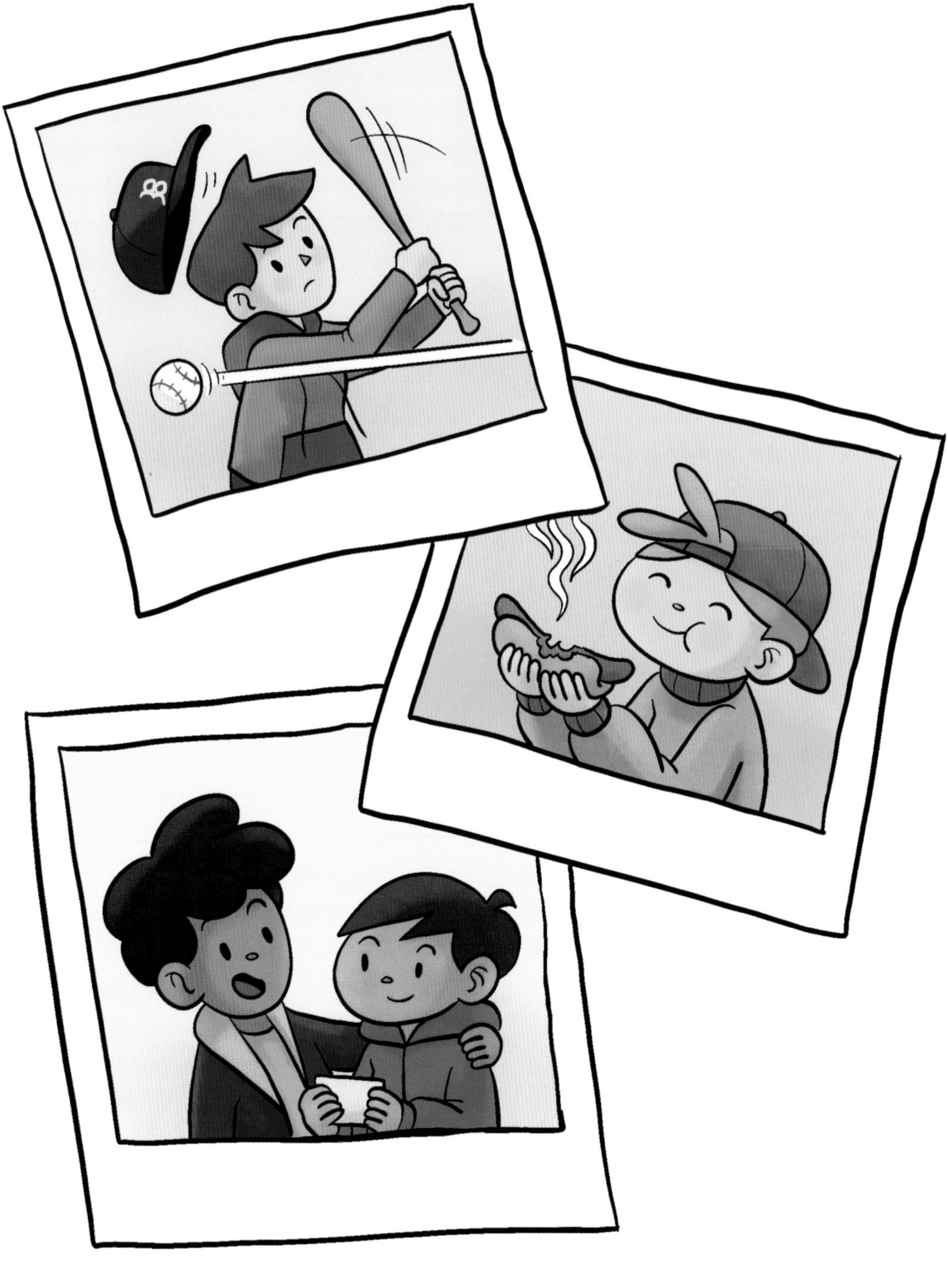

Contents

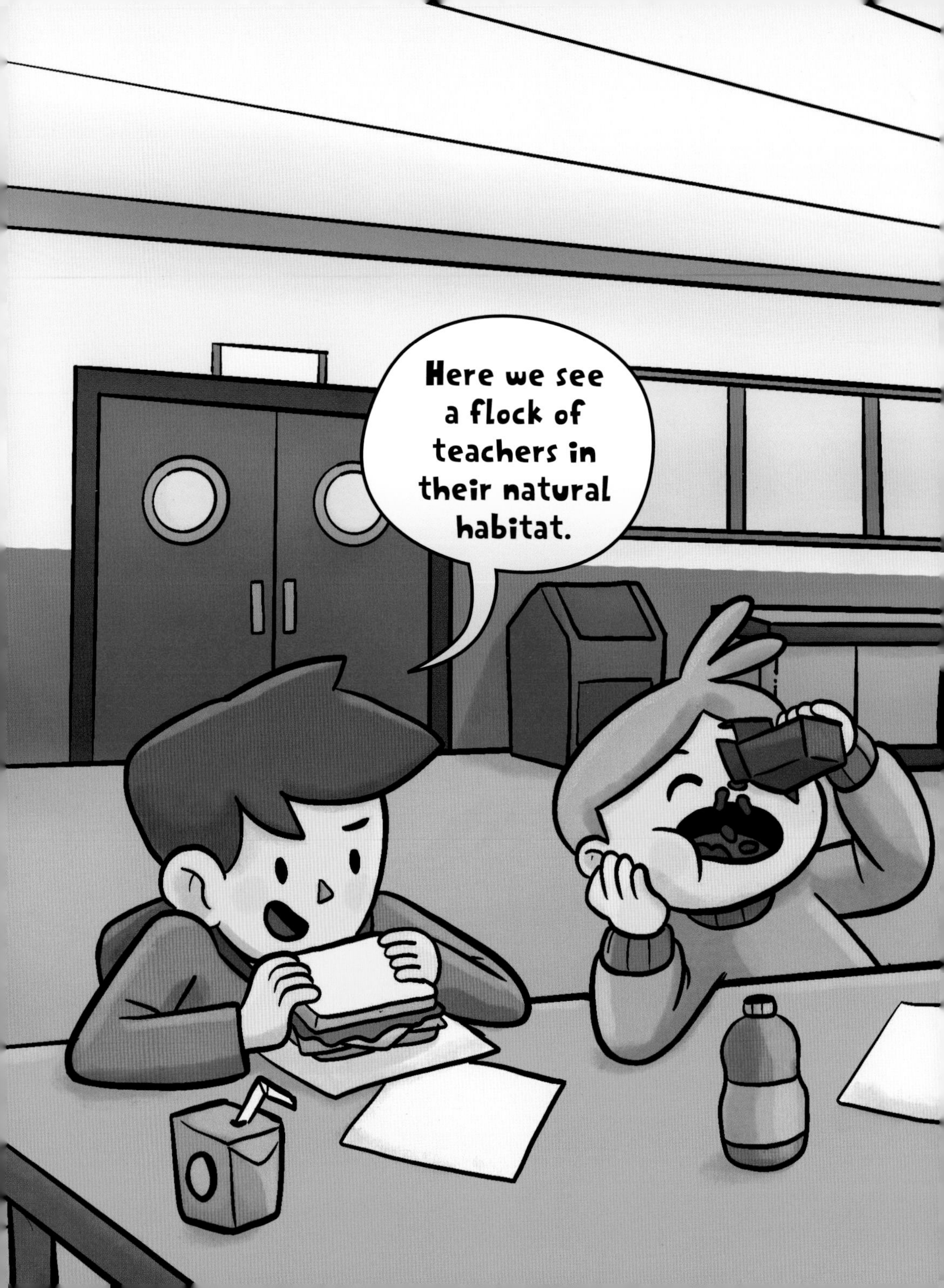
Here we see a flock of teachers in their natural habitat.

CHAPTER ONE

No Girls Allowed

Lucky peered over a giant sandwich at a group of teachers eating lunch in the cafeteria.

Red pounded on a painfully empty box of raisins.

"What do you think they're talking about?" Lucky pondered, pretending to be the host on his very own nature show.

"Perhaps about their lives," Red suggested.

"I bet they are saying, 'I am so lucky to have Lucky in my class!'"

"I am sure they are," Red said, rolling his eyes.

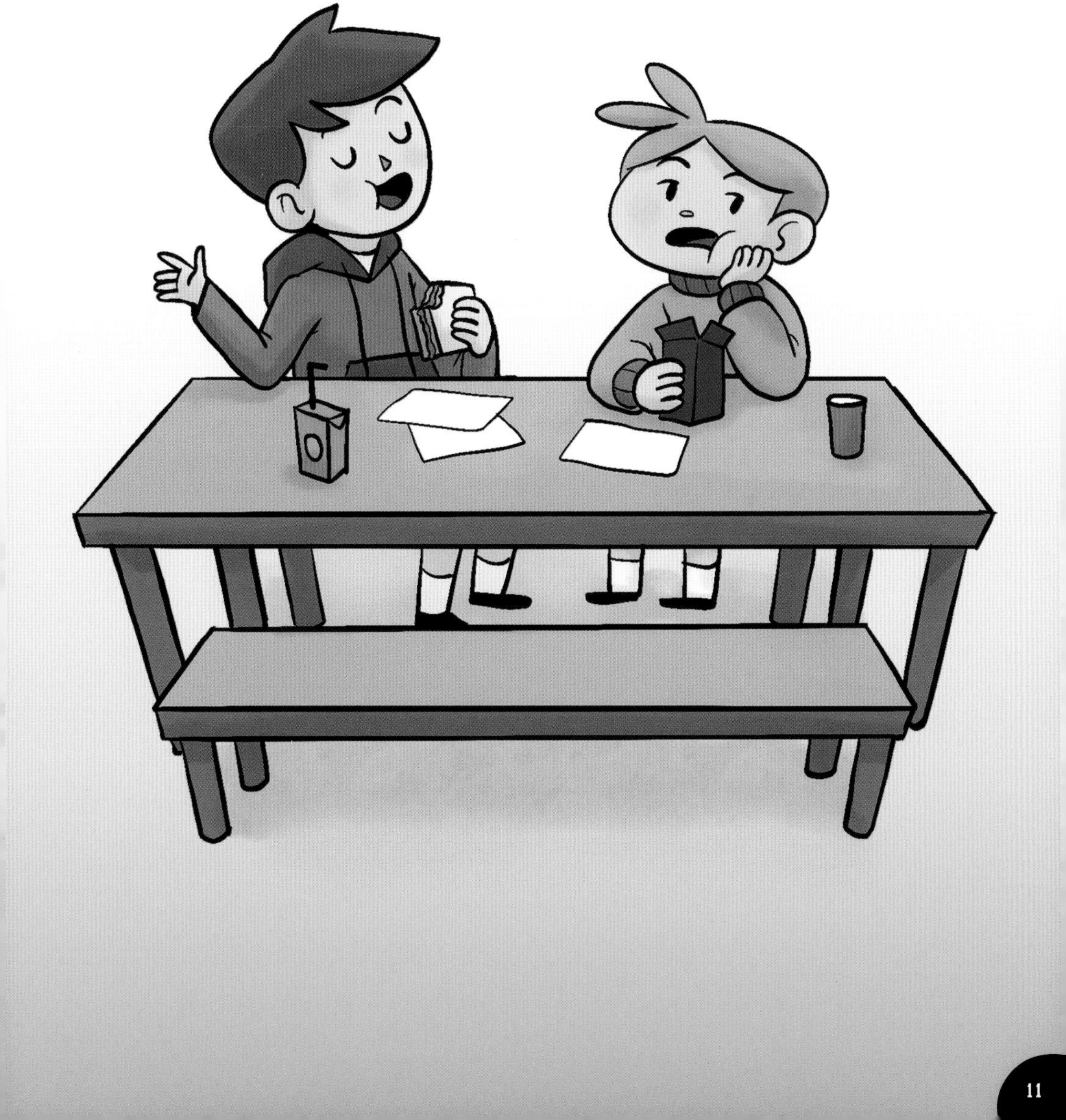

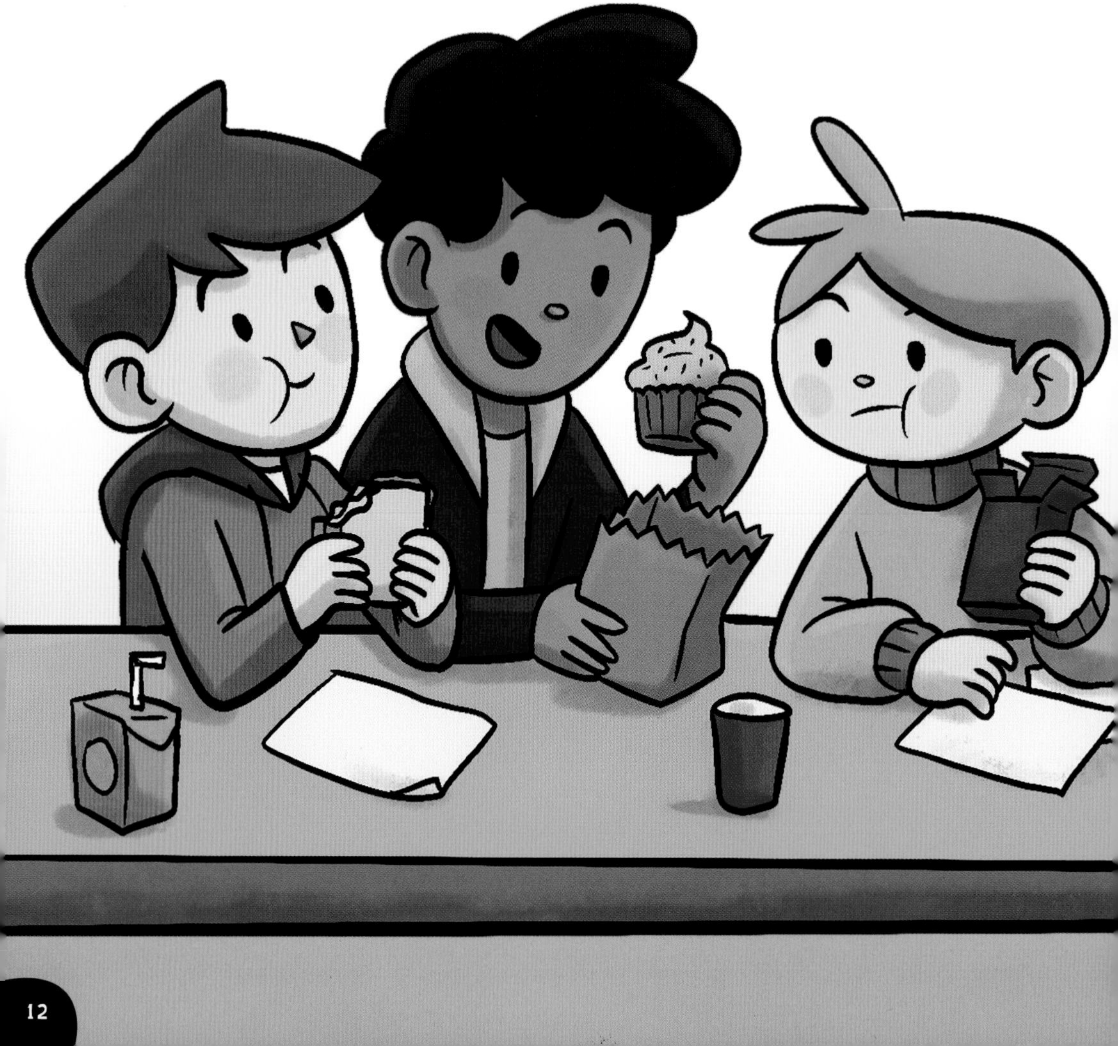

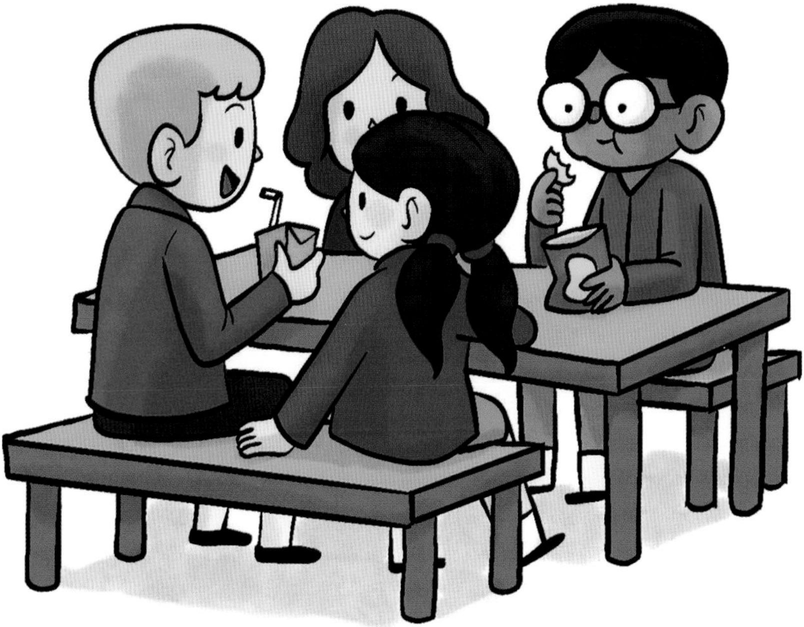

"Hey, guys!" Rudy squeezed in between Red and Lucky with his brown paper bag. He took out a cupcake the size of a baseball. "What did you all think of class today? Marty and Rosie's presentation was the best."

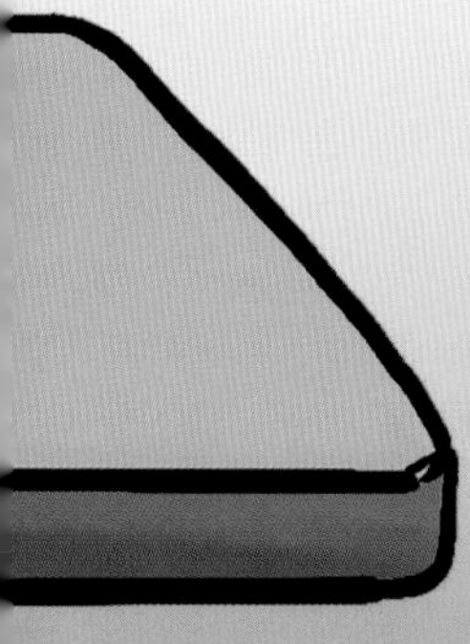

"They always have the best presentations," Red agreed, but he was staring at the giant cupcake with envy.

"Well, they *are* best friends," said Lucky. "Imagine how great it would be if they let the three of *us* work together." The boys banged on their table and laughed.

They would **NEVER** let **THAT** happen.

"It helps that Rosie's a girl," said Lucky. "The teachers never suspect she and Marty are best friends. We should ask Rosie about that."

"There she is!" said Red. The boys ran over to her.

"You had a really great presentation in class today," said Rudy. "It must be great to work with your best friend."

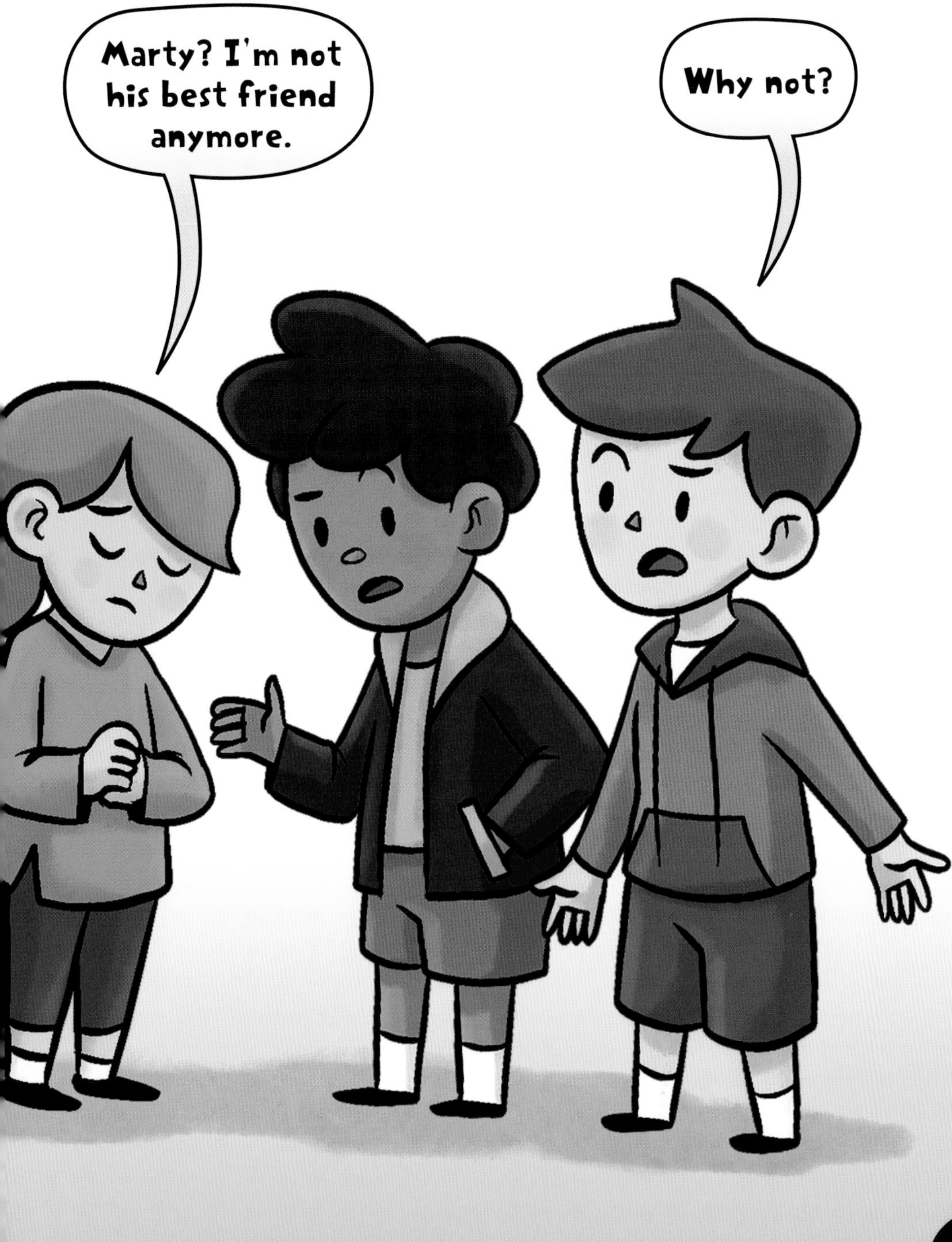
Marty? I'm not his best friend anymore.
Why not?

"He didn't invite me to his birthday party," Rosie said. The boys hurriedly hid their invitations.

"Why didn't he?" Lucky asked.

"He said that the other boys wouldn't allow him to be best friends with a girl anymore. Don't tell him I told you!" Rosie pleaded.

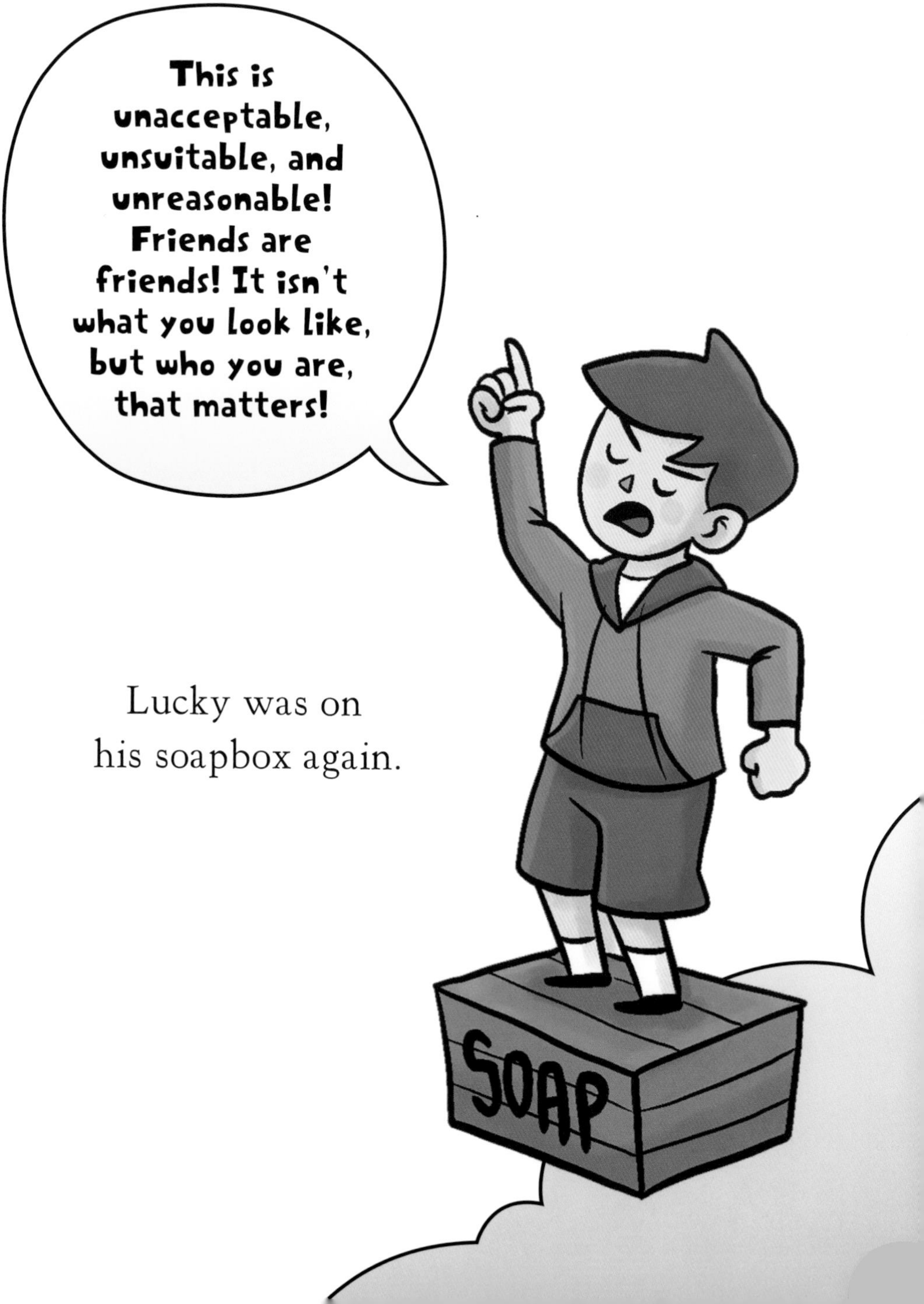
This is unacceptable, unsuitable, and unreasonable! Friends are friends! It isn't what you look like, but who you are, that matters!
SOAP

Lucky was on
his soapbox again.

It was Mrs. Gogolak. Rudy and Red inched away.

Lucky climbed down, walked over to the gang, and whispered, “This is a job for the Good Guys Agency!”

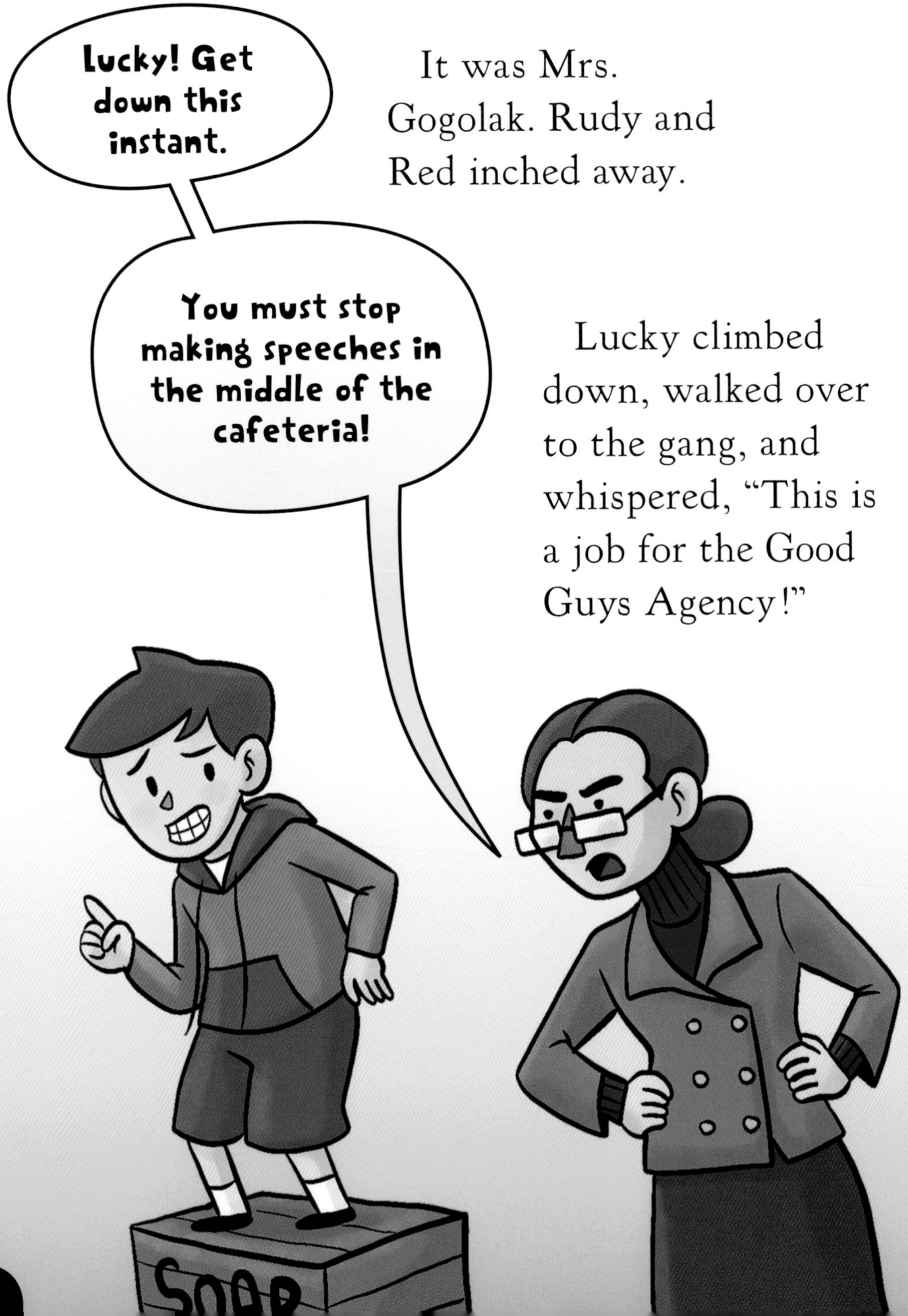
Lucky! Get down this instant.
You must stop making speeches in the middle of the cafeteria!

"Yes!" Rudy said with a fist pump.

"Everyone to their stations," Lucky instructed. "Let's go!"

"But it's only lunch. We have to be here for another three hours," Rudy said.

"Okay. New plan," said Lucky. "We will go to class and *then* another class and *one* last one. *Then* we will pack up our things, get on the bus, drive home, and *then* we will GO TO OUR STATIONS!"

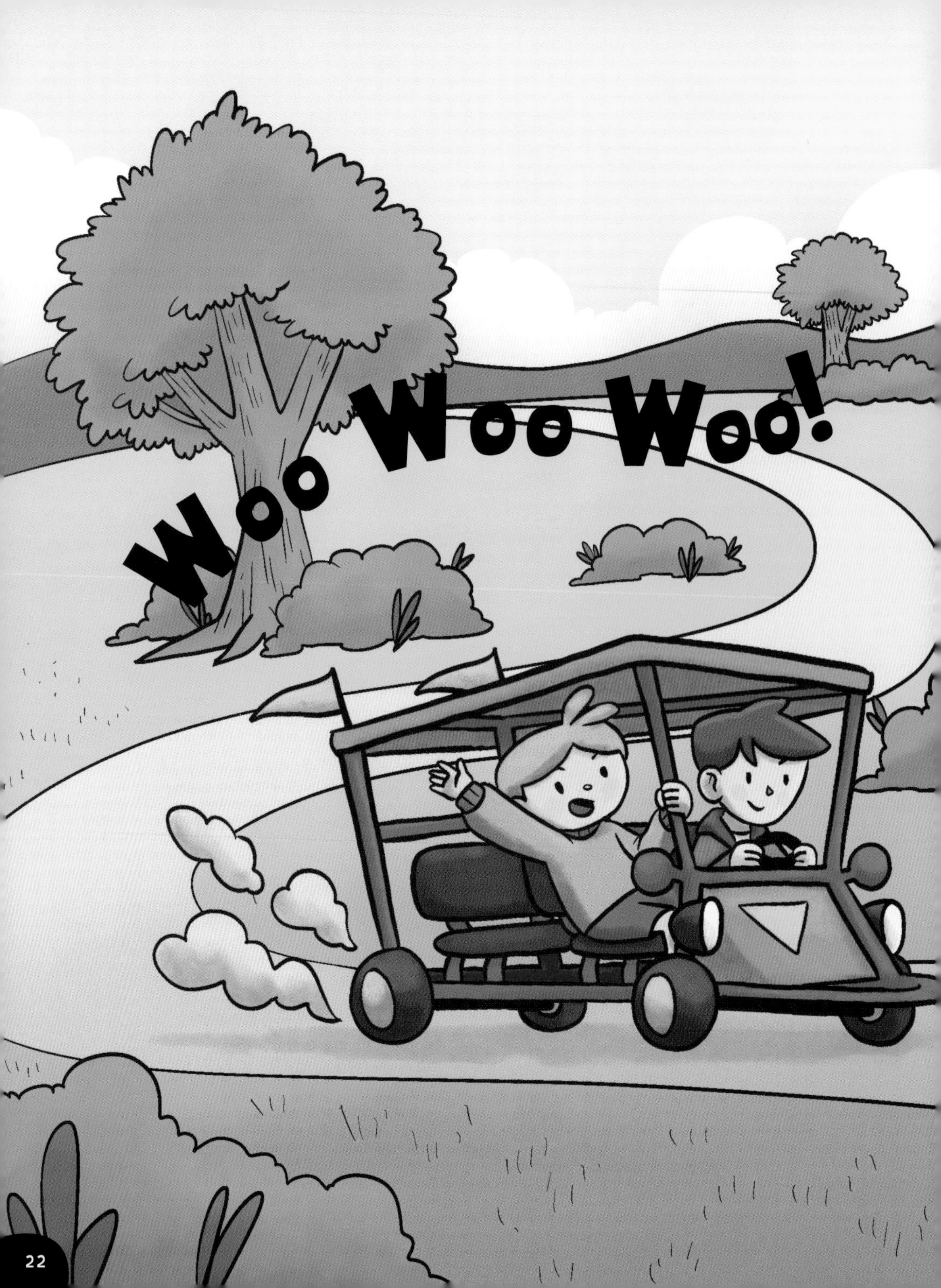
Woo Woo Woo!

CHAPTER TWO

The Case of the Missing Invitation

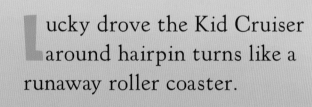

Lucky drove the Kid Cruiser around hairpin turns like a runaway roller coaster.

They pulled up to a house and knocked on a big green door.

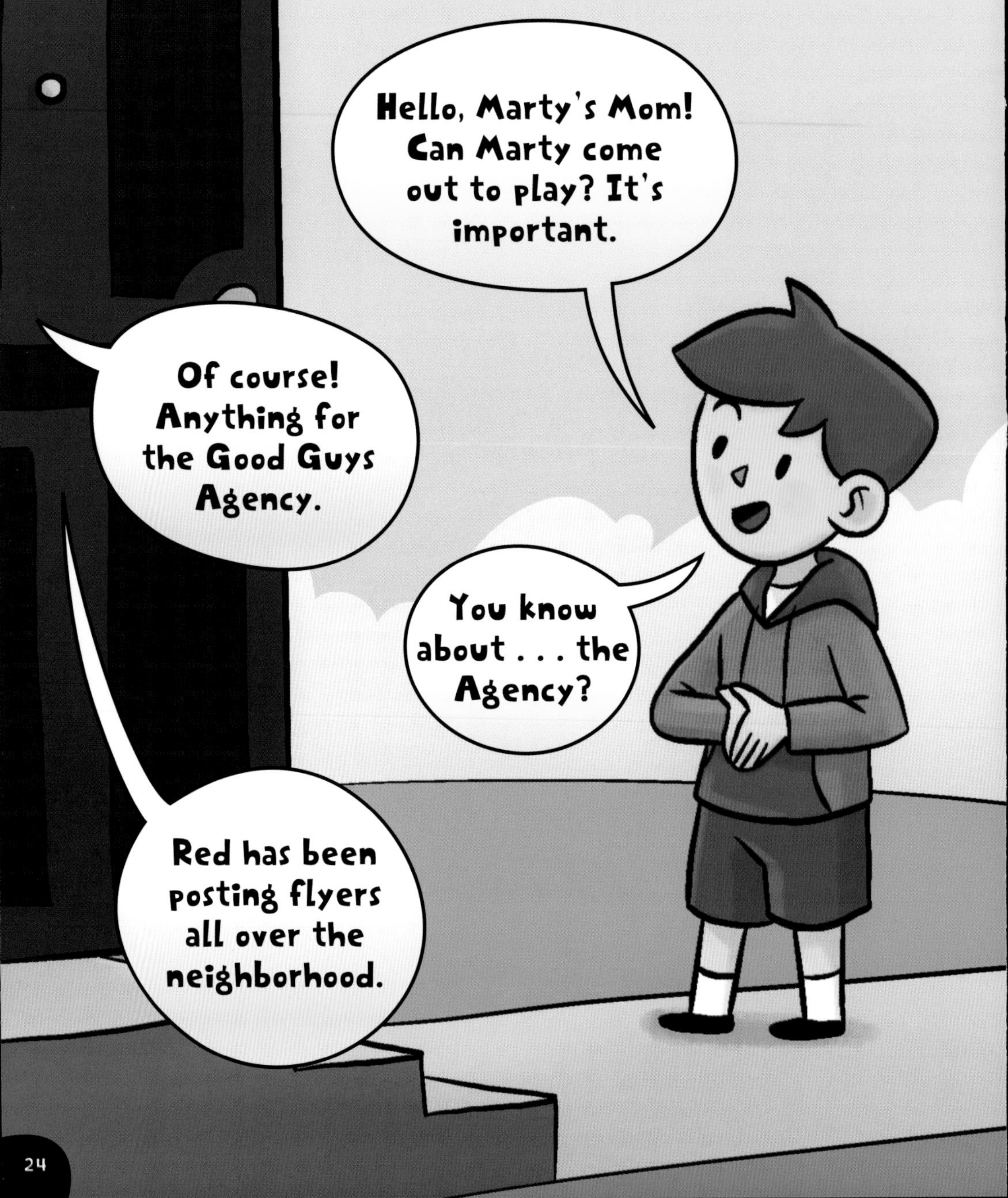
Hello, Marty's Mom! Can Marty come out to play? It's important.
Of course! Anything for the Good Guys Agency.
You know about . . . the Agency?
Red has been posting flyers all over the neighborhood.

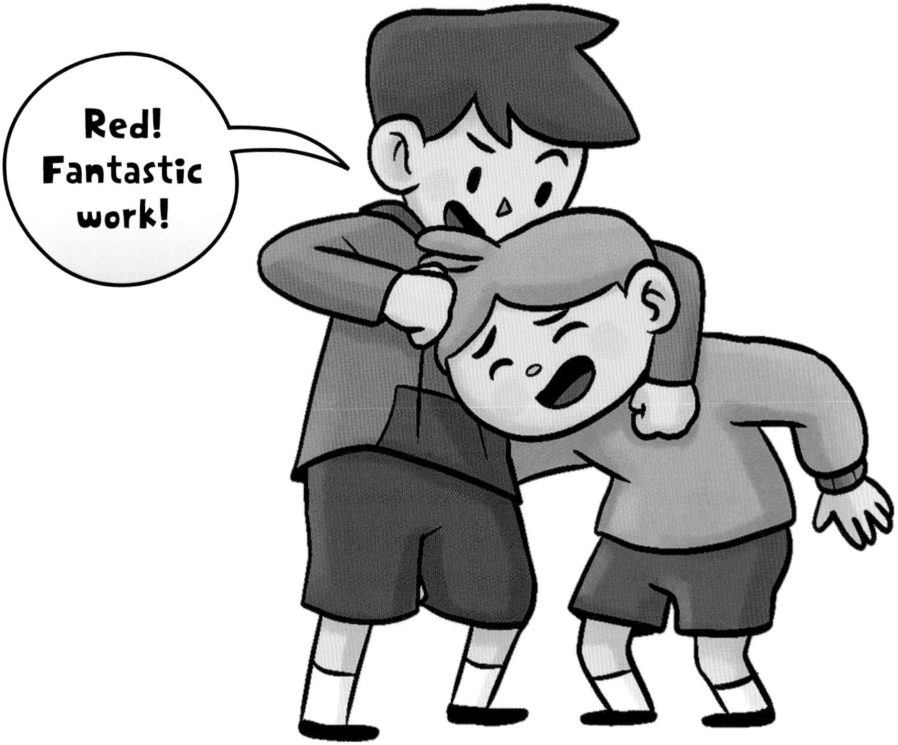
Red! Fantastic work!

The three boys ran to the Kid Cruiser to start the adventure, their destination still a mystery.

"What's all this about?" Marty asked.

"It's about your party, Marty . . . Party, Marty . . . that rhymes!" Lucky giggled. "We have a client who is upset about the invitation situation . . . I did it again—I can't stop it!"

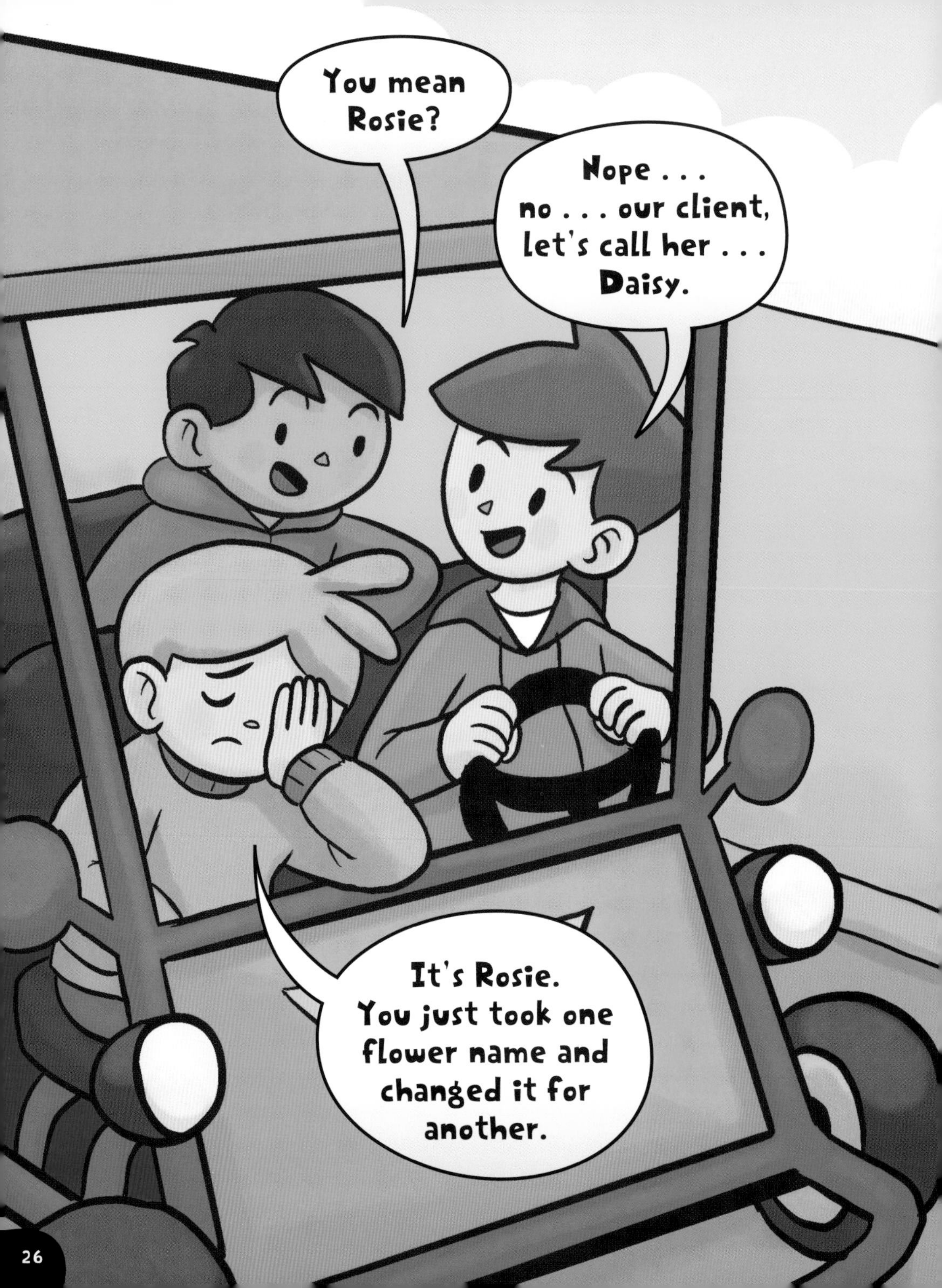
You mean Rosie?
Nope . . . no . . . our client, let's call her . . . Daisy.
It's Rosie. You just took one flower name and changed it for another.

"Don't you still want her to be your friend?" Red asked.

"Of course I do," said Marty, "but I am scared to stand up to all the guys at school."

"Sounds like we just need to get you some courage," Lucky said.

Lucky, Lucky, come in! Are you ready? I have the perfect hero for courage: Jackie Robinson!

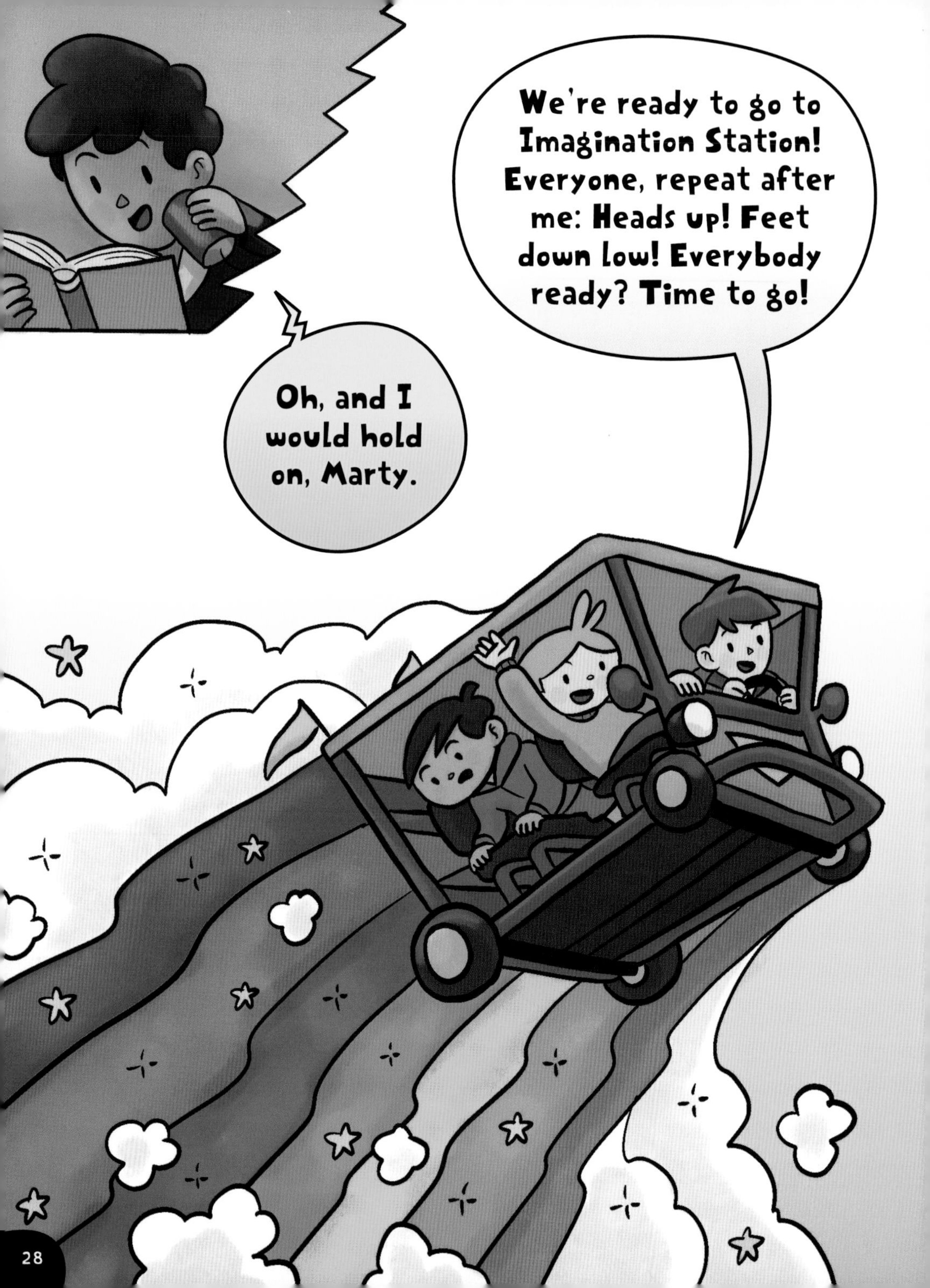
We're ready to go to Imagination Station! Everyone, repeat after me: Heads up! Feet down low! Everybody ready? Time to go!
Oh, and I would hold on, Marty.

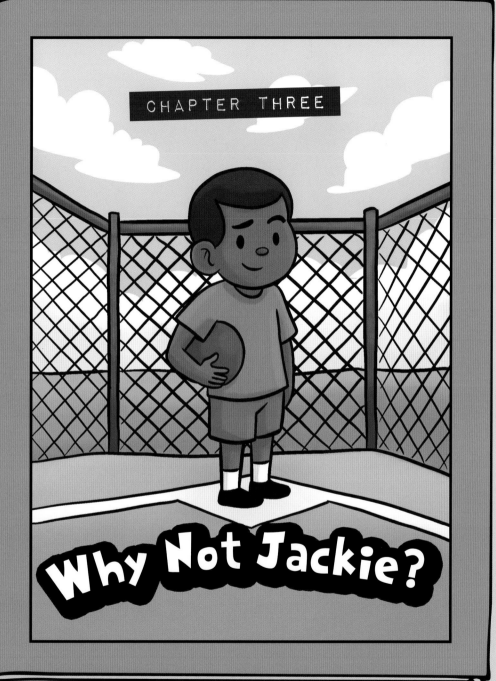

CHAPTER THREE

Why Not Jackie?

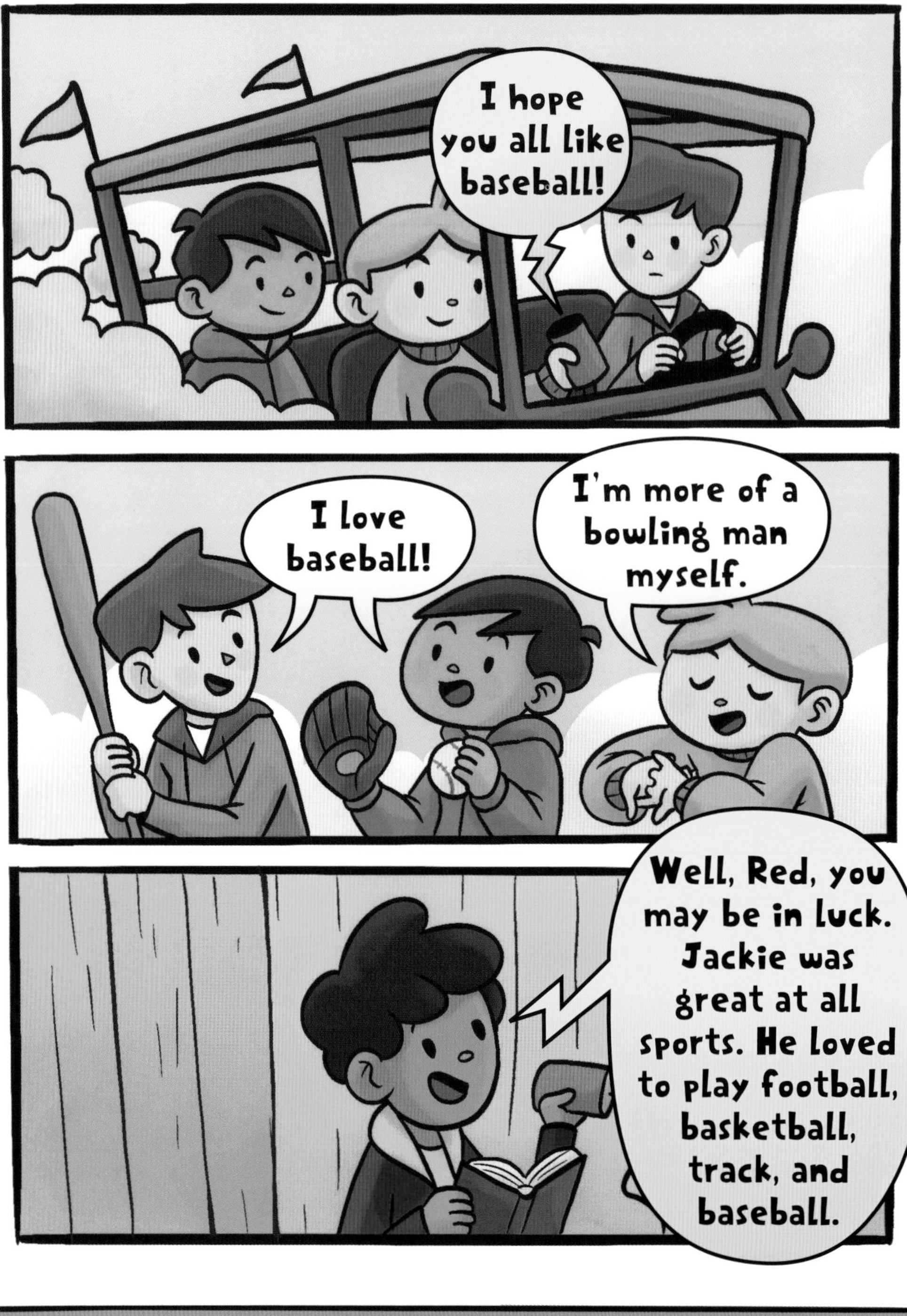
I hope you all like baseball!
I love baseball!
I'm more of a bowling man myself.
Well, Red, you may be in luck. Jackie was great at all sports. He loved to play football, basketball, track, and baseball.

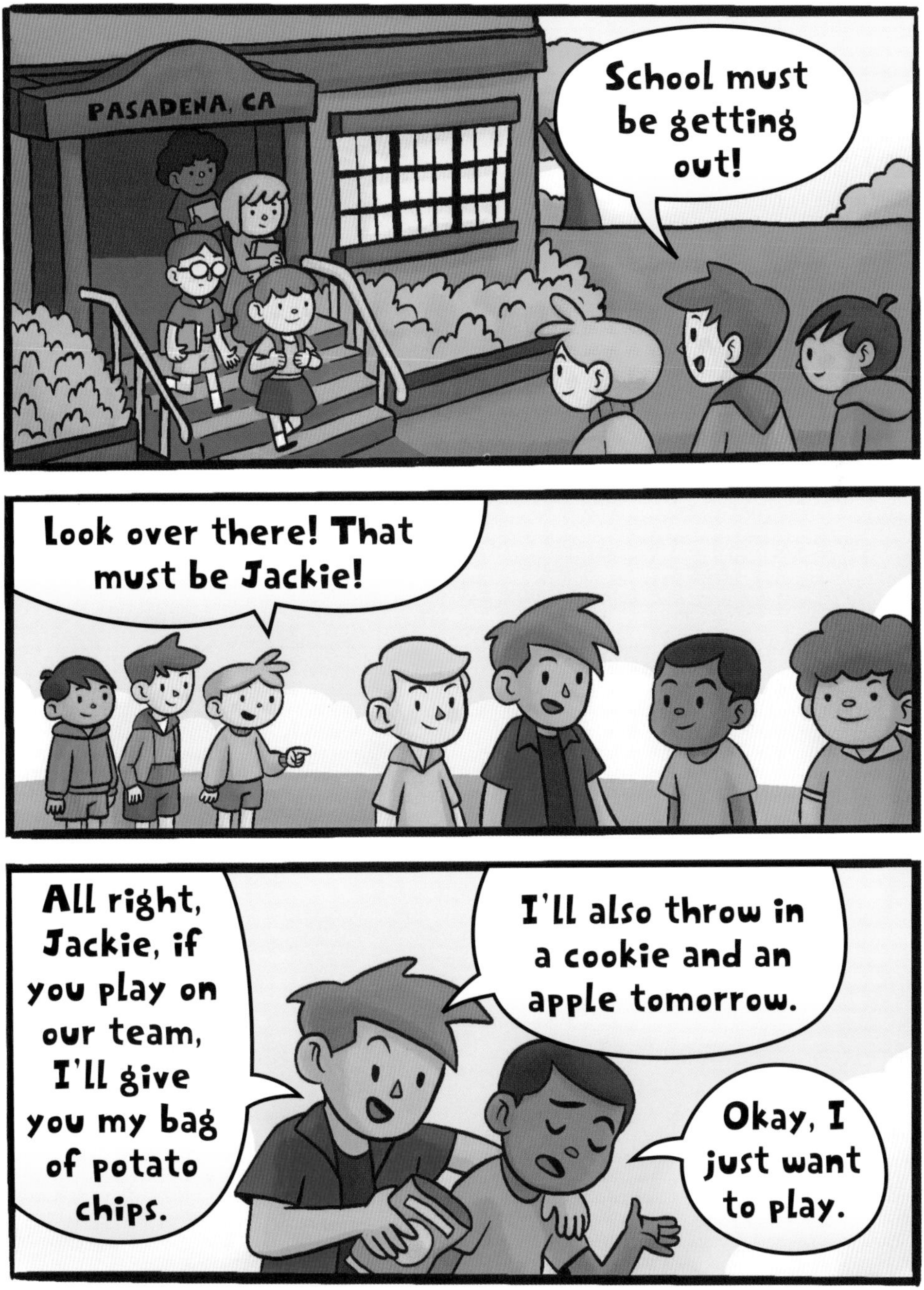
PASADENA, CA
School must be getting out!
Look over there! That must be Jackie!
All right, Jackie, if you play on our team, I'll give you my bag of potato chips.
I'll also throw in a cookie and an apple tomorrow.
Okay, I just want to play.

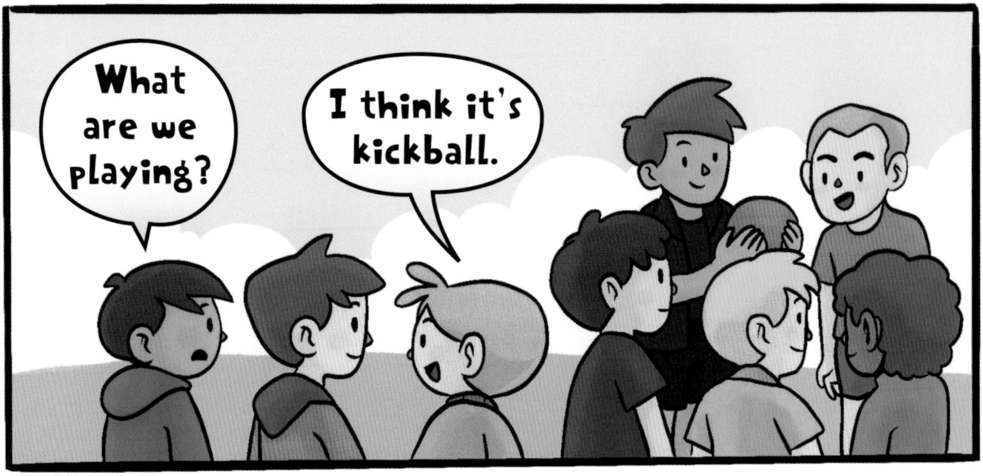
What are we playing?
I think it's kickball.

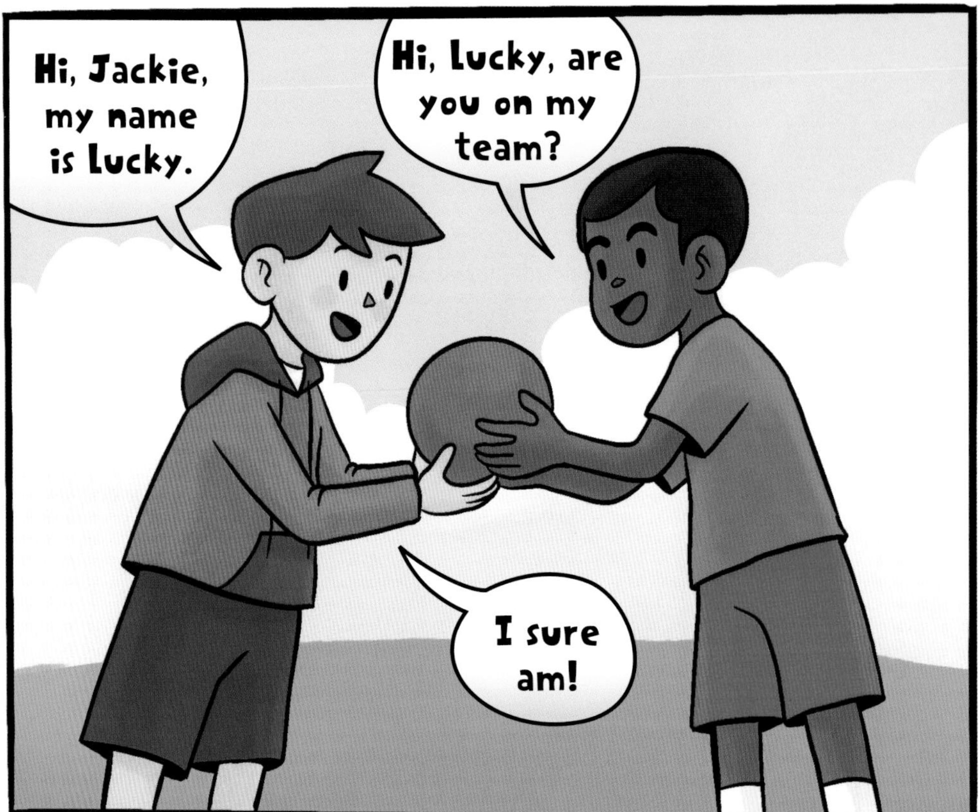
Hi, Jackie, my name is Lucky.
Hi, Lucky, are you on my team?
I sure am!

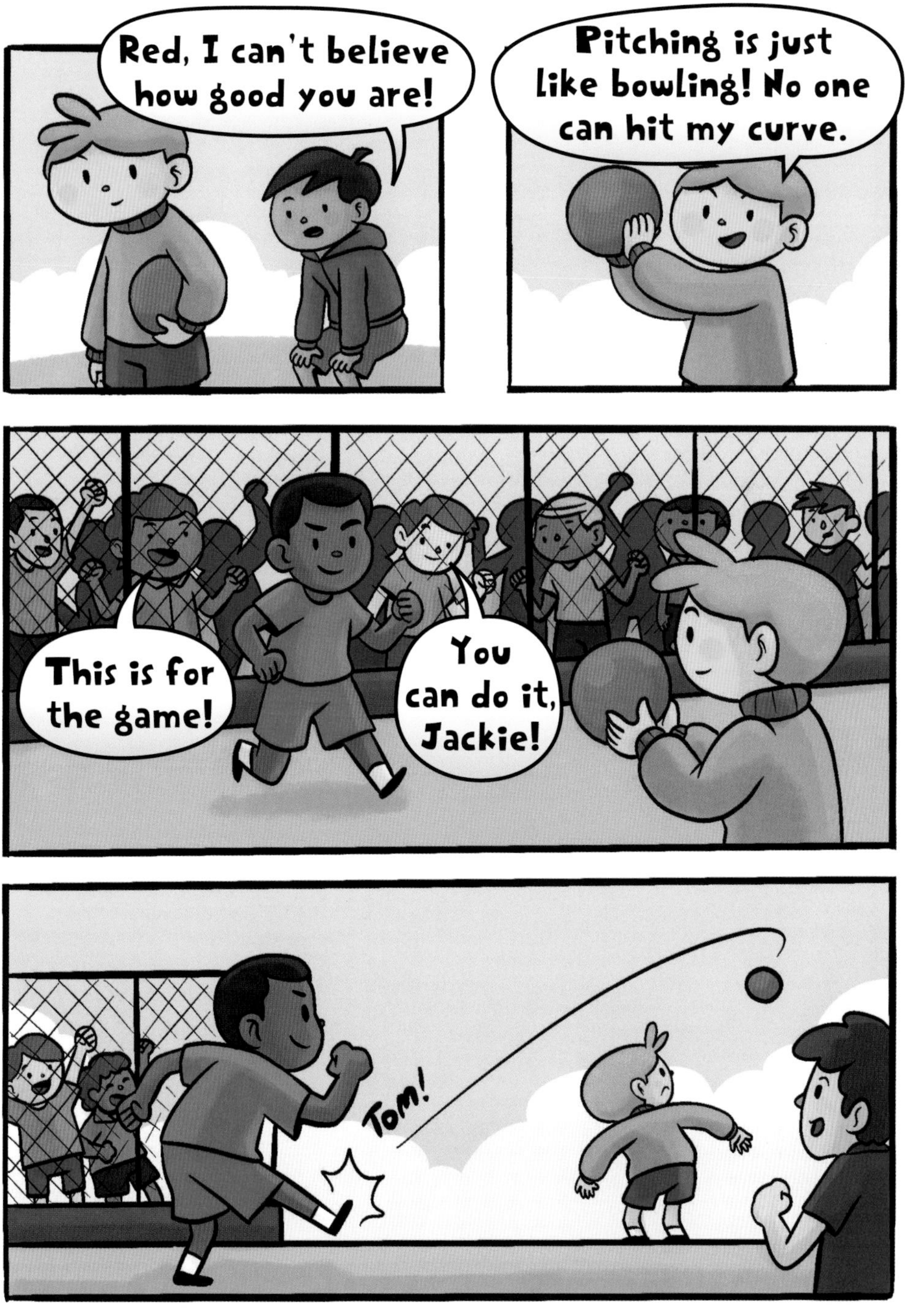
Red, I can't believe how good you are!
Pitching is just like bowling! No one can hit my curve.
This is for the game!
You can do it, Jackie!
Tom!

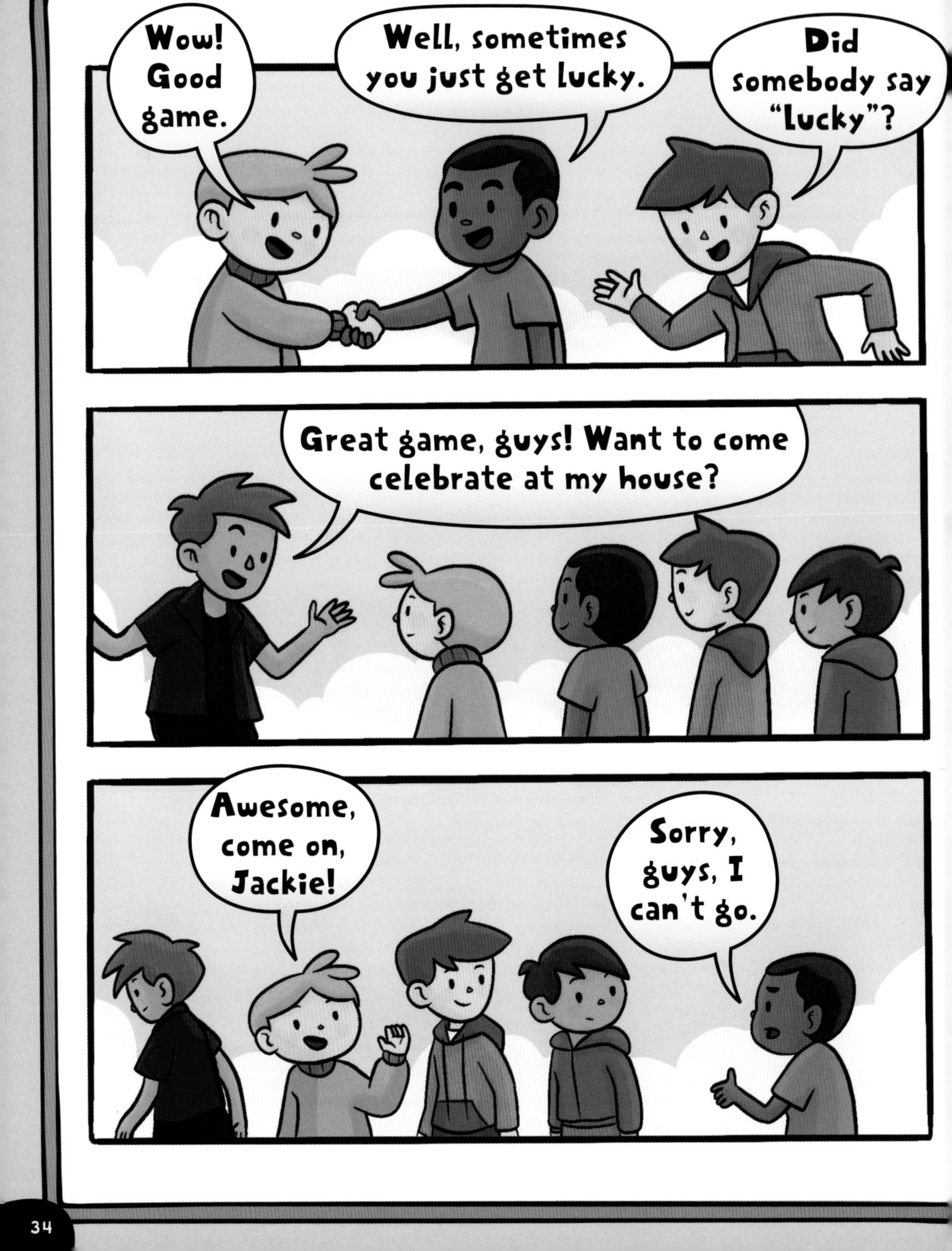
Wow! Good game.
Well, sometimes you just get lucky.
Did somebody say "Lucky"?
Great game, guys! Want to come celebrate at my house?
Awesome, come on, Jackie!
Sorry, guys, I can't go.

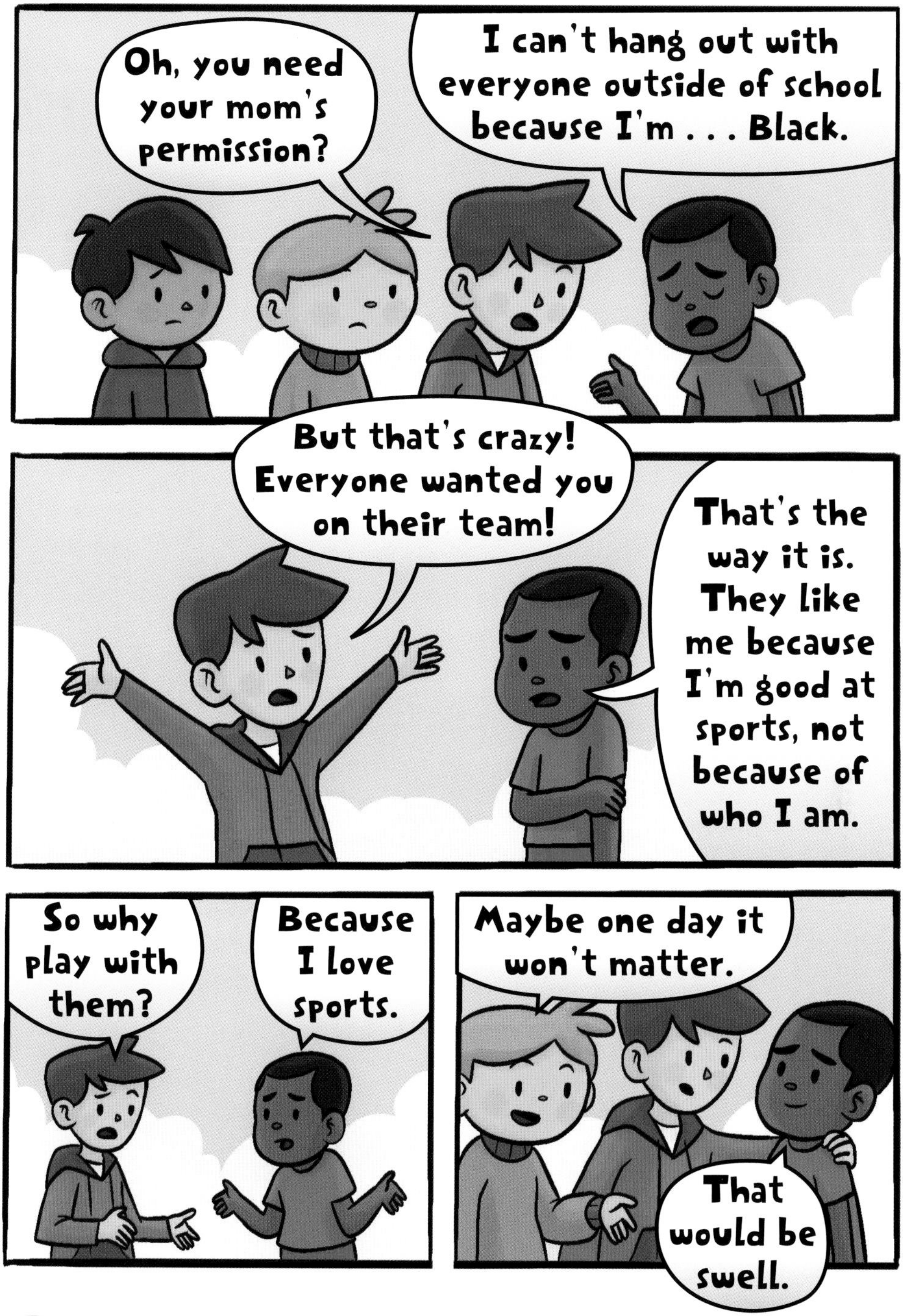
Oh, you need your mom's permission?
I can't hang out with everyone outside of school because I'm . . . Black.
But that's crazy! Everyone wanted you on their team!
That's the way it is. They like me because I'm good at sports, not because of who I am.
So why play with them?
Because I love sports.
Maybe one day it won't matter.
That would be swell.

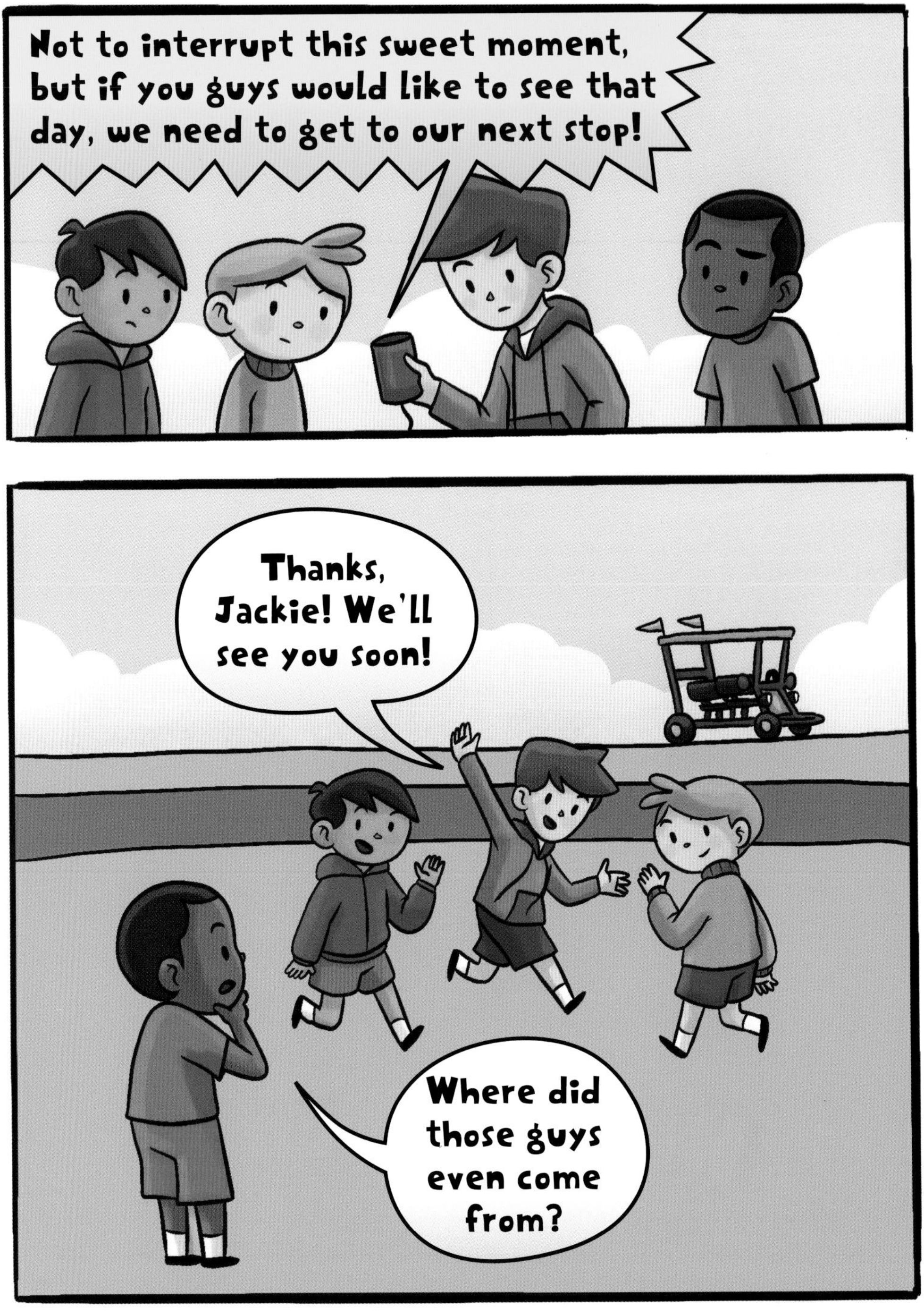
Not to interrupt this sweet moment, but if you guys would like to see that day, we need to get to our next stop!
Thanks, Jackie! We'll see you soon!
Where did those guys even come from?

CHAPTER FOUR

Headed Home

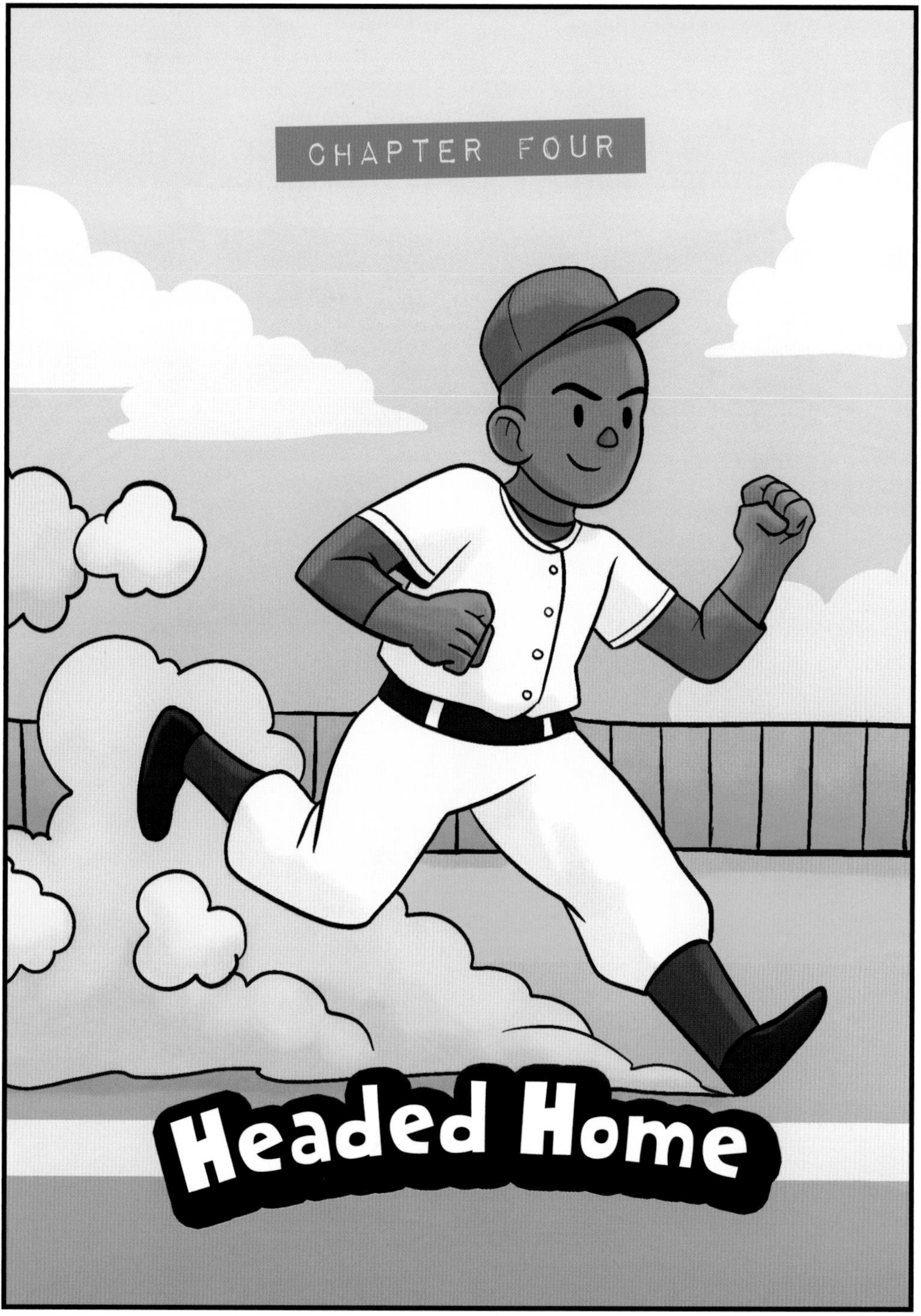

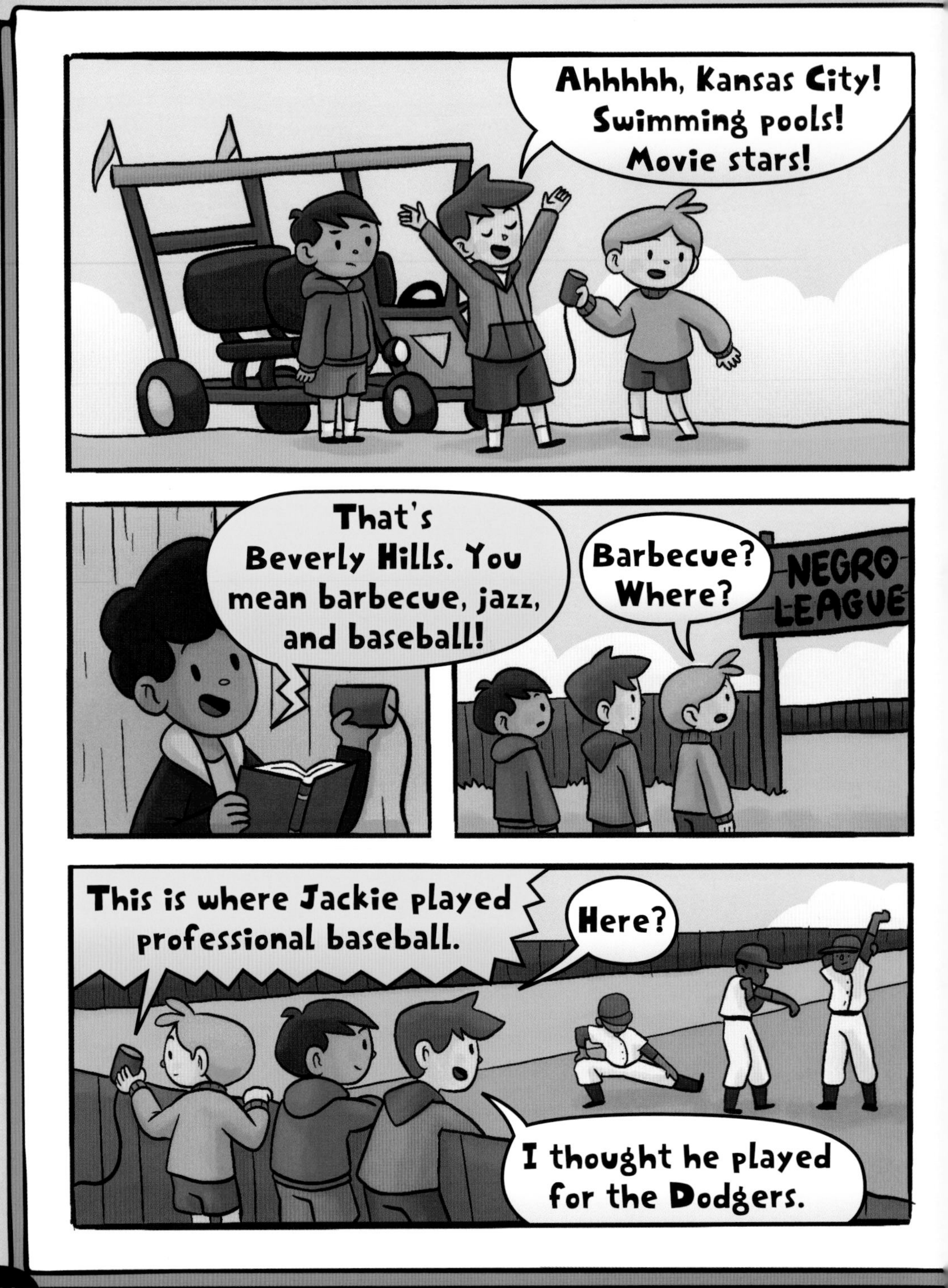
Ahhhhh, Kansas City! Swimming pools! Movie stars!
That's Beverly Hills. You mean barbecue, jazz, and baseball!
Barbecue? Where?
NEGRO LEAGUE
This is where Jackie played professional baseball.
Here?
I thought he played for the Dodgers.

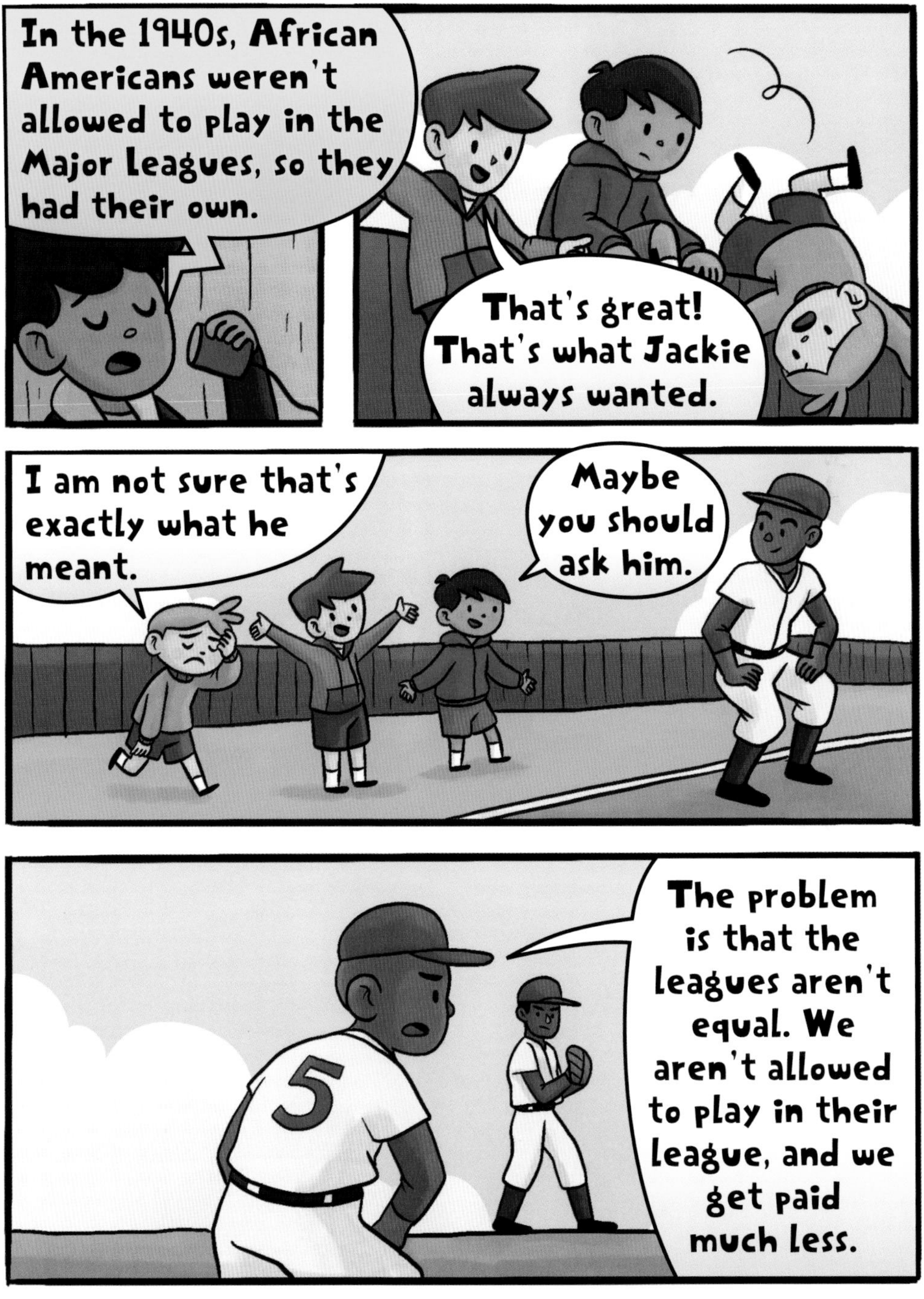
In the 1940s, African Americans weren't allowed to play in the Major Leagues, so they had their own.
That's great! That's what Jackie always wanted.
I am not sure that's exactly what he meant.
Maybe you should ask him.
The problem is that the leagues aren't equal. We aren't allowed to play in their league, and we get paid much less.

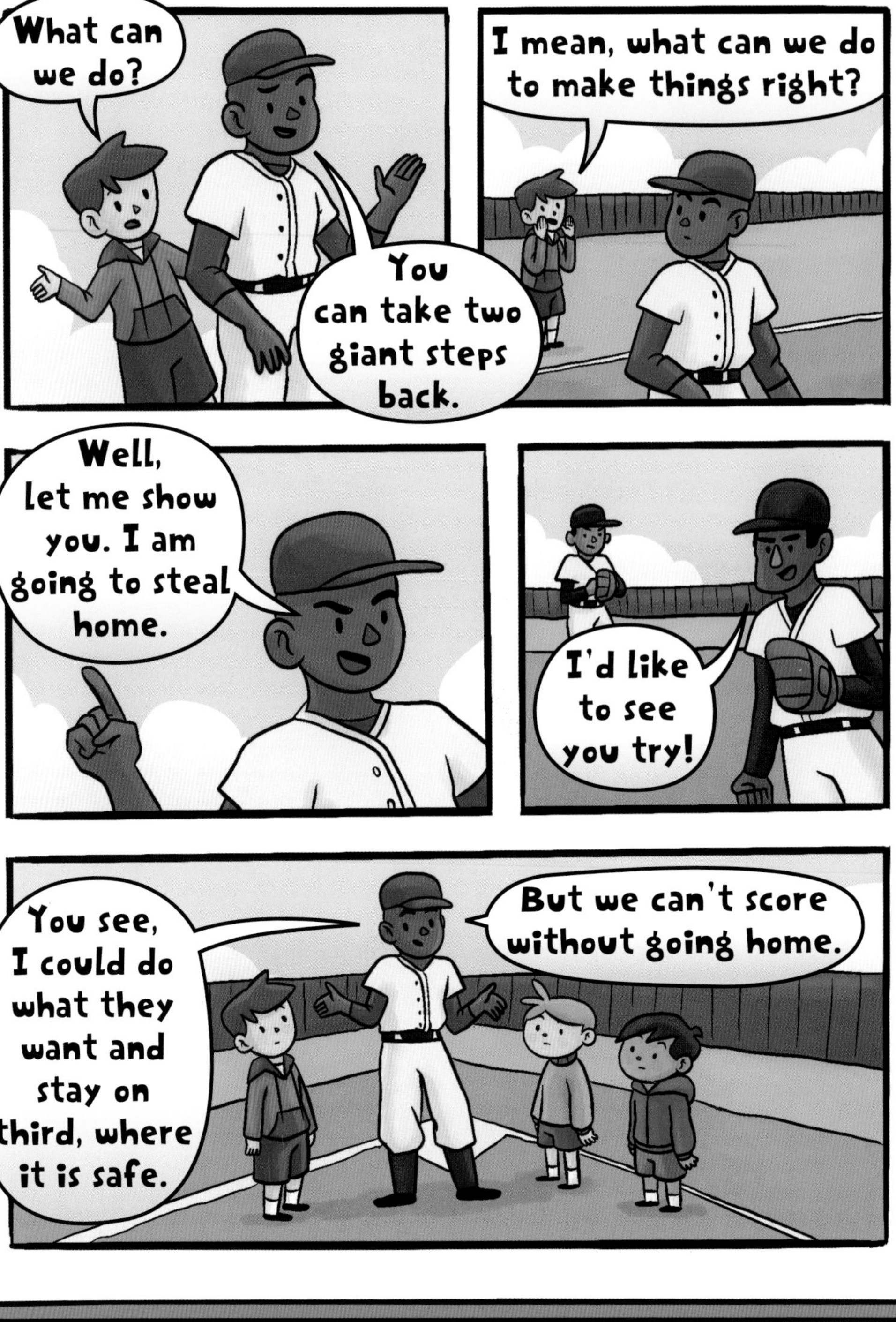
What can we do?
You can take two giant steps back.
I mean, what can we do to make things right?
Well, let me show you. I am going to steal home.
I'd like to see you try!
You see, I could do what they want and stay on third, where it is safe.
But we can't score without going home.

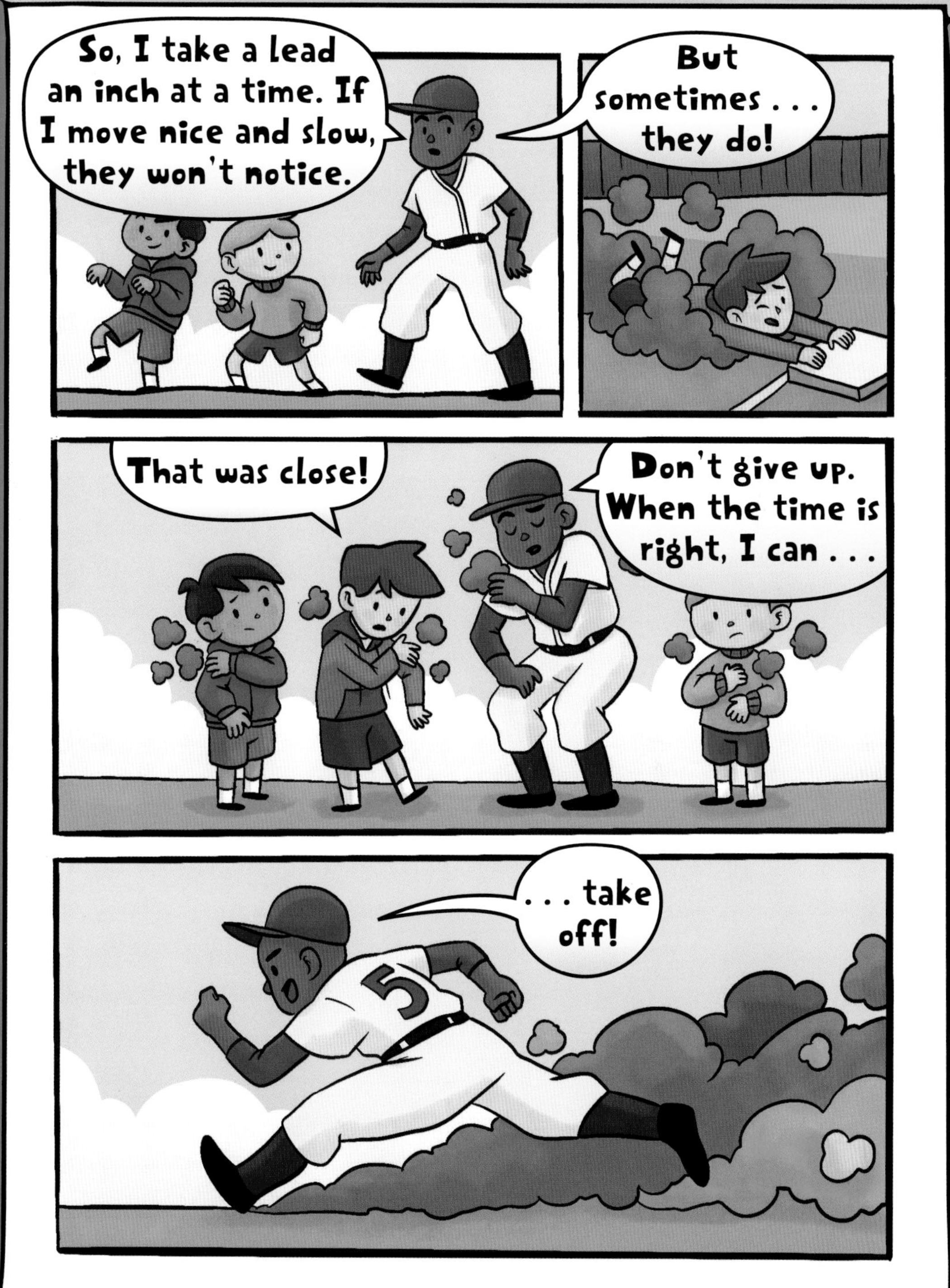
So, I take a lead an inch at a time. If I move nice and slow, they won't notice.
But sometimes . . . they do!
That was close!
Don't give up. When the time is right, I can . . .
. . . take off!

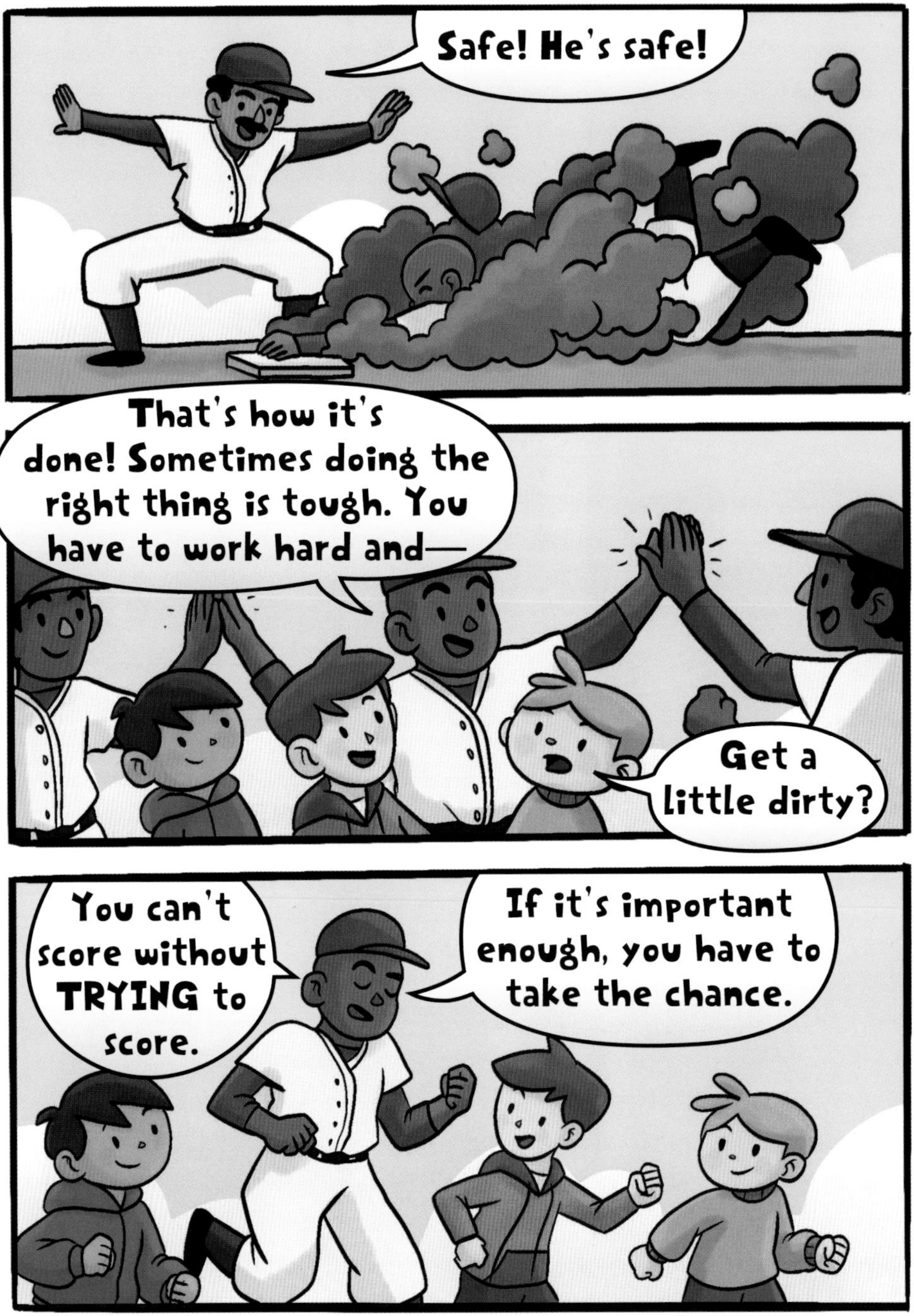
Safe! He's safe!
That's how it's done! Sometimes doing the right thing is tough. You have to work hard and—
Get a little dirty?
You can't score without TRYING to score.
If it's important enough, you have to take the chance.

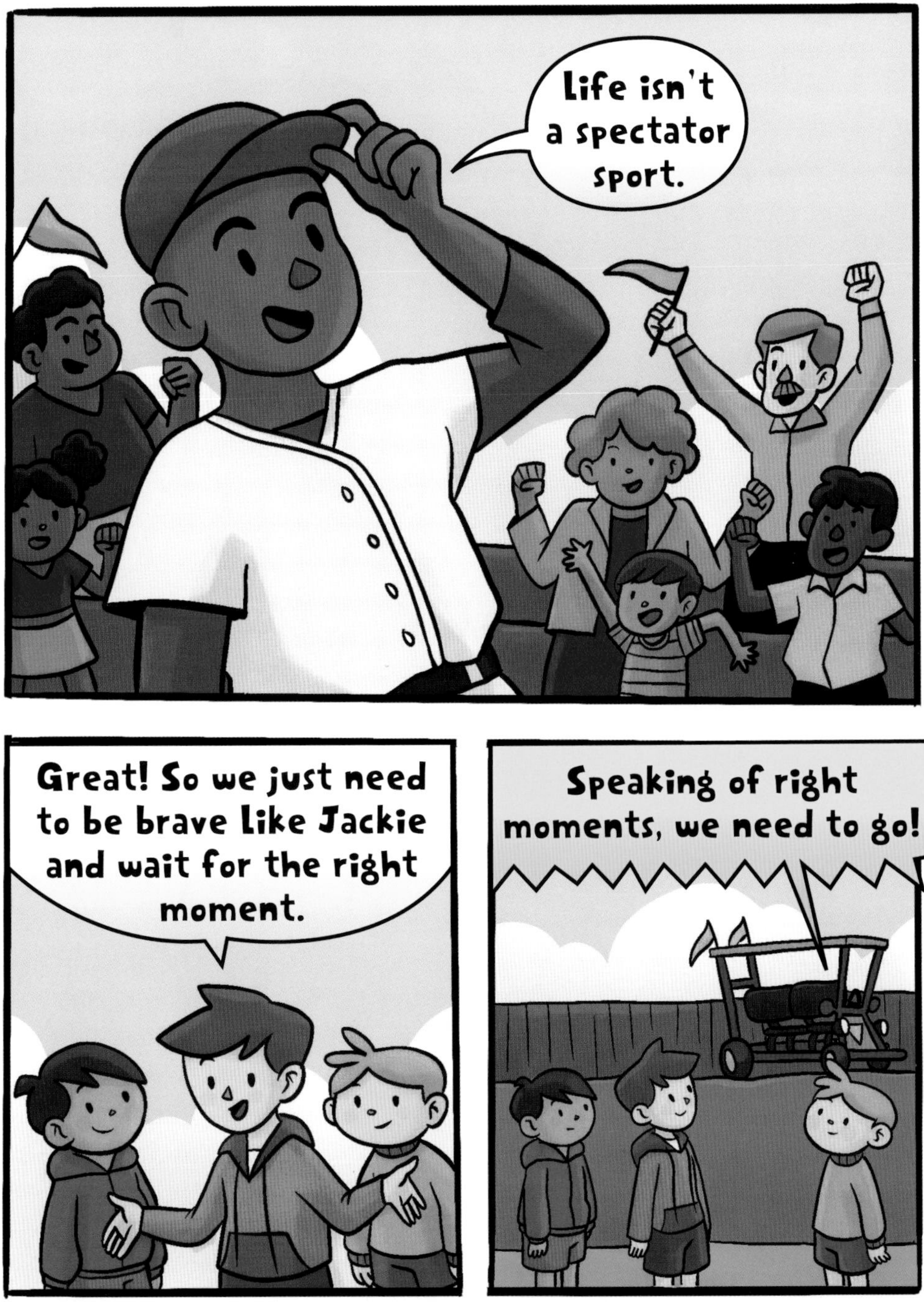
Life isn't a spectator sport.
Great! So we just need to be brave like Jackie and wait for the right moment.
Speaking of right moments, we need to go!

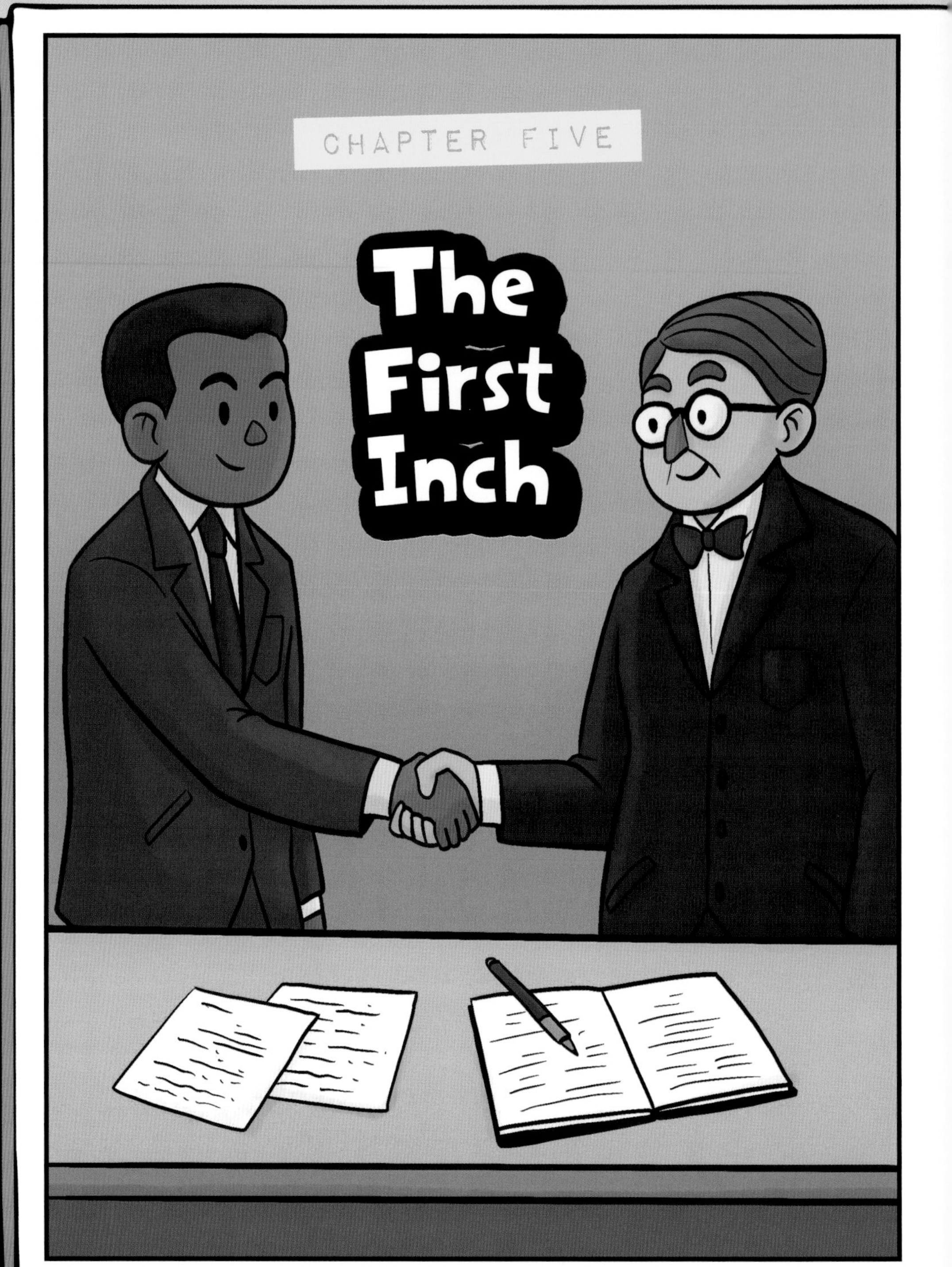
CHAPTER FIVE
The First Inch

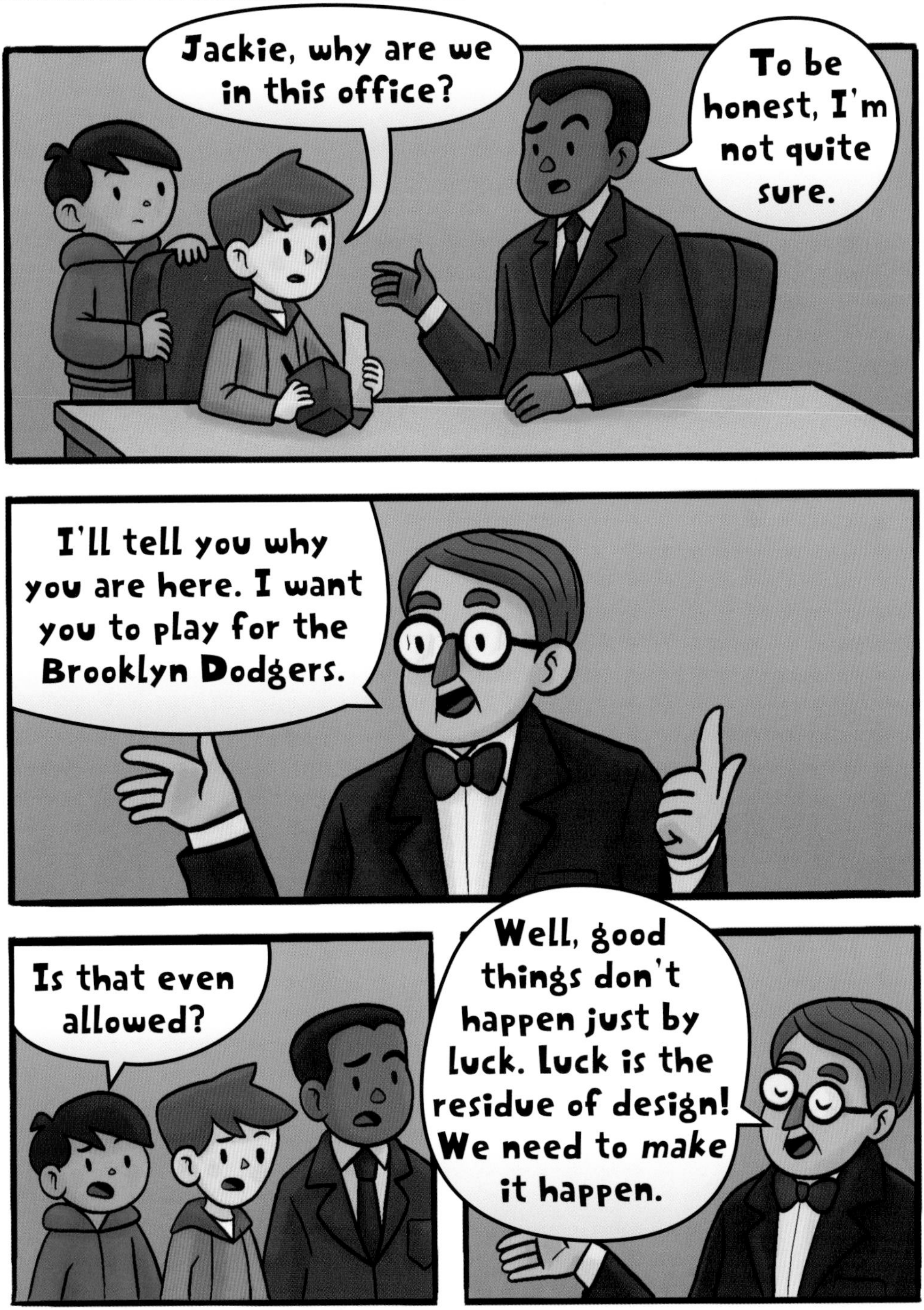
Jackie, why are we in this office?
To be honest, I'm not quite sure.
I'll tell you why you are here. I want you to play for the Brooklyn Dodgers.
Is that even allowed?
Well, good things don't happen just by luck. Luck is the residue of design! We need to *make* it happen.

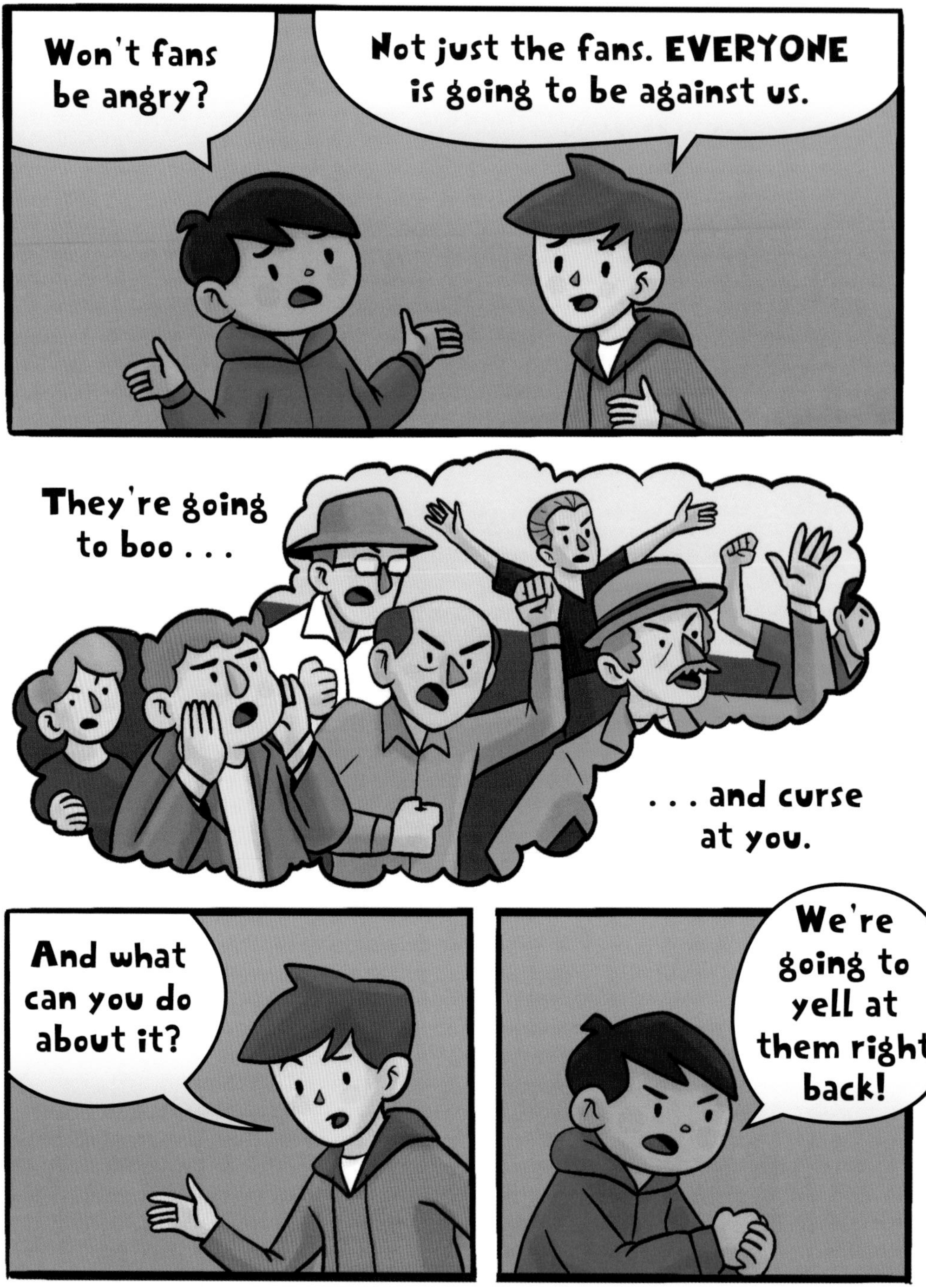
Won't fans be angry?
Not just the fans. EVERYONE is going to be against us.
They're going to boo . . .
. . . and curse at you.
And what can you do about it?
We're going to yell at them right back!

No! That's what they want. If he acts crazy, he'll be the first and **LAST** Black player.

I need you to have enough guts not to fight. Problems are the price you pay for progress.

Progress I can do.

But I don't look like your other players.

Can you hit? Can you run? Are you a good person?

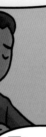

I sure can!

Then you look exactly the way that I want you to look.

A great ballplayer is one who will take a chance.

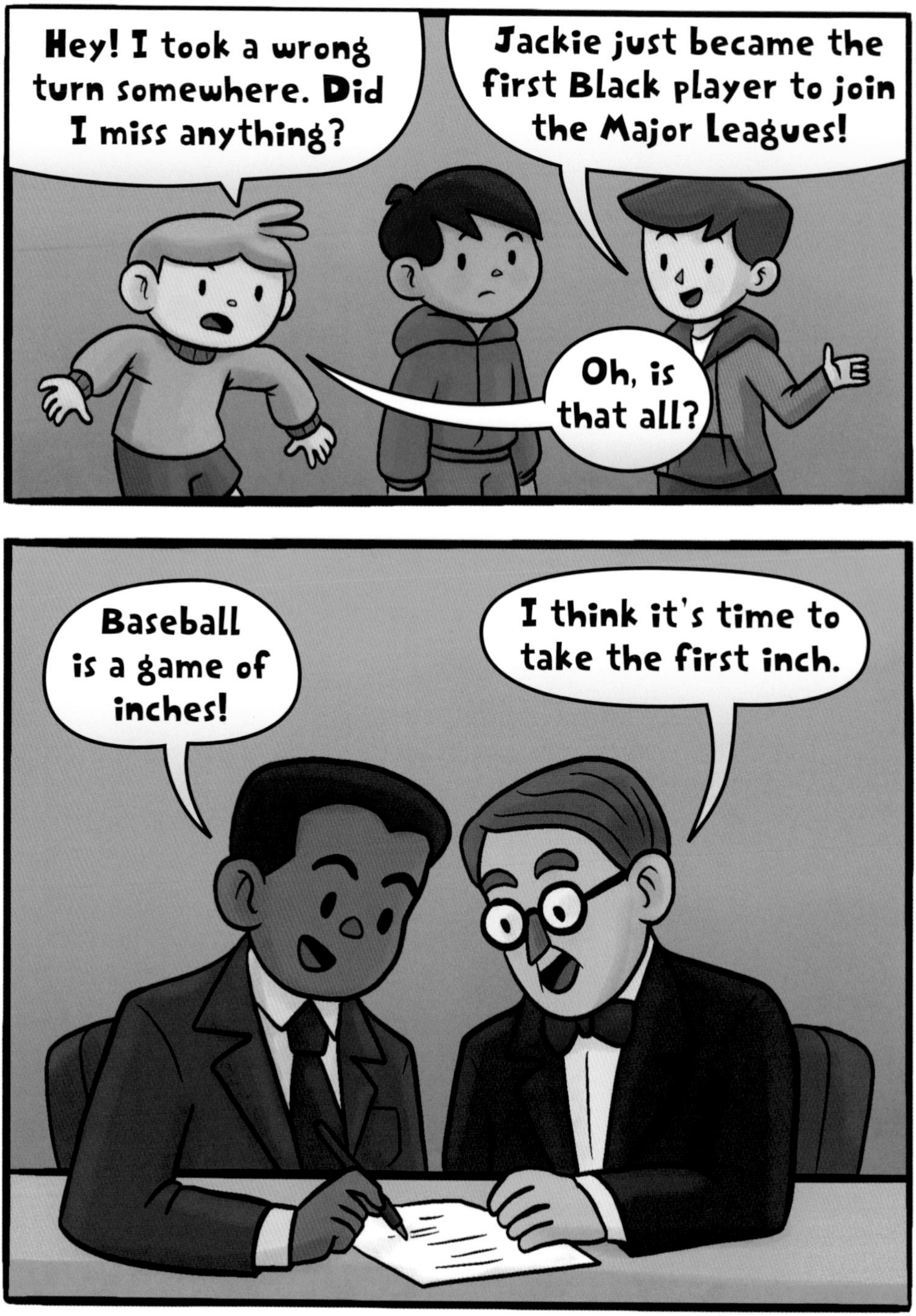

Hey! I took a wrong turn somewhere. Did I miss anything?
Jackie just became the first Black player to join the Major Leagues!
Oh, is that all?
Baseball is a game of inches!
I think it's time to take the first inch.

CHAPTER SIX

The Number 42

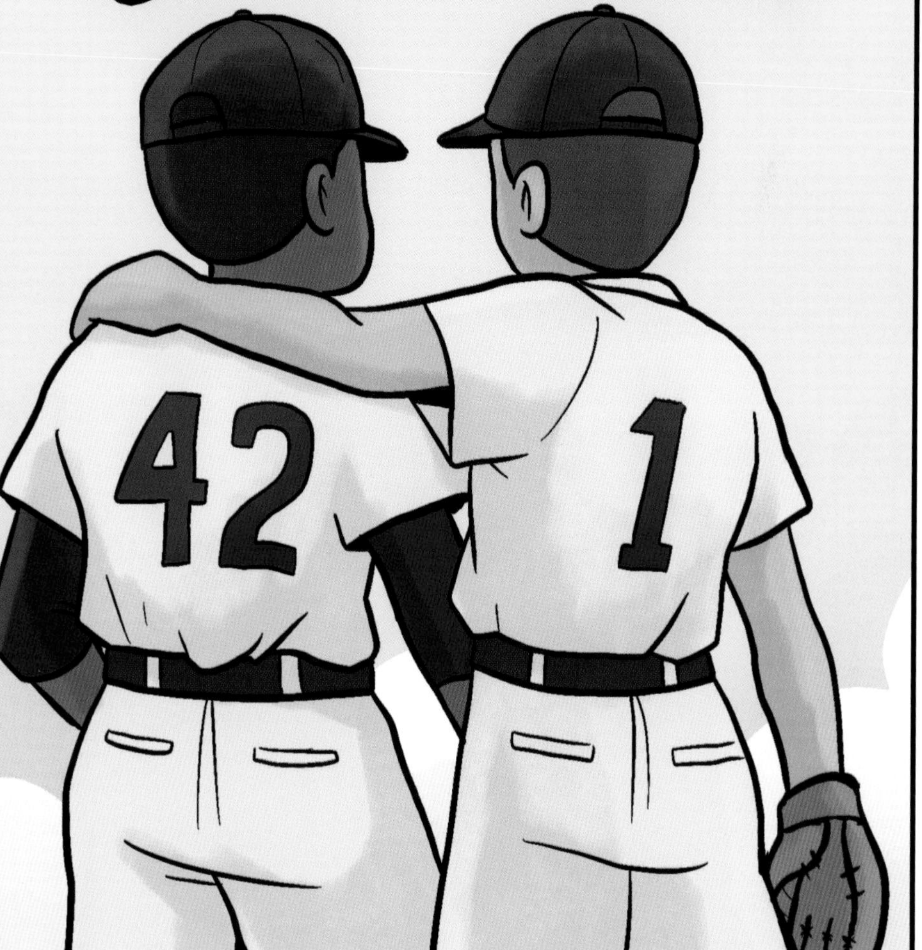
42
1

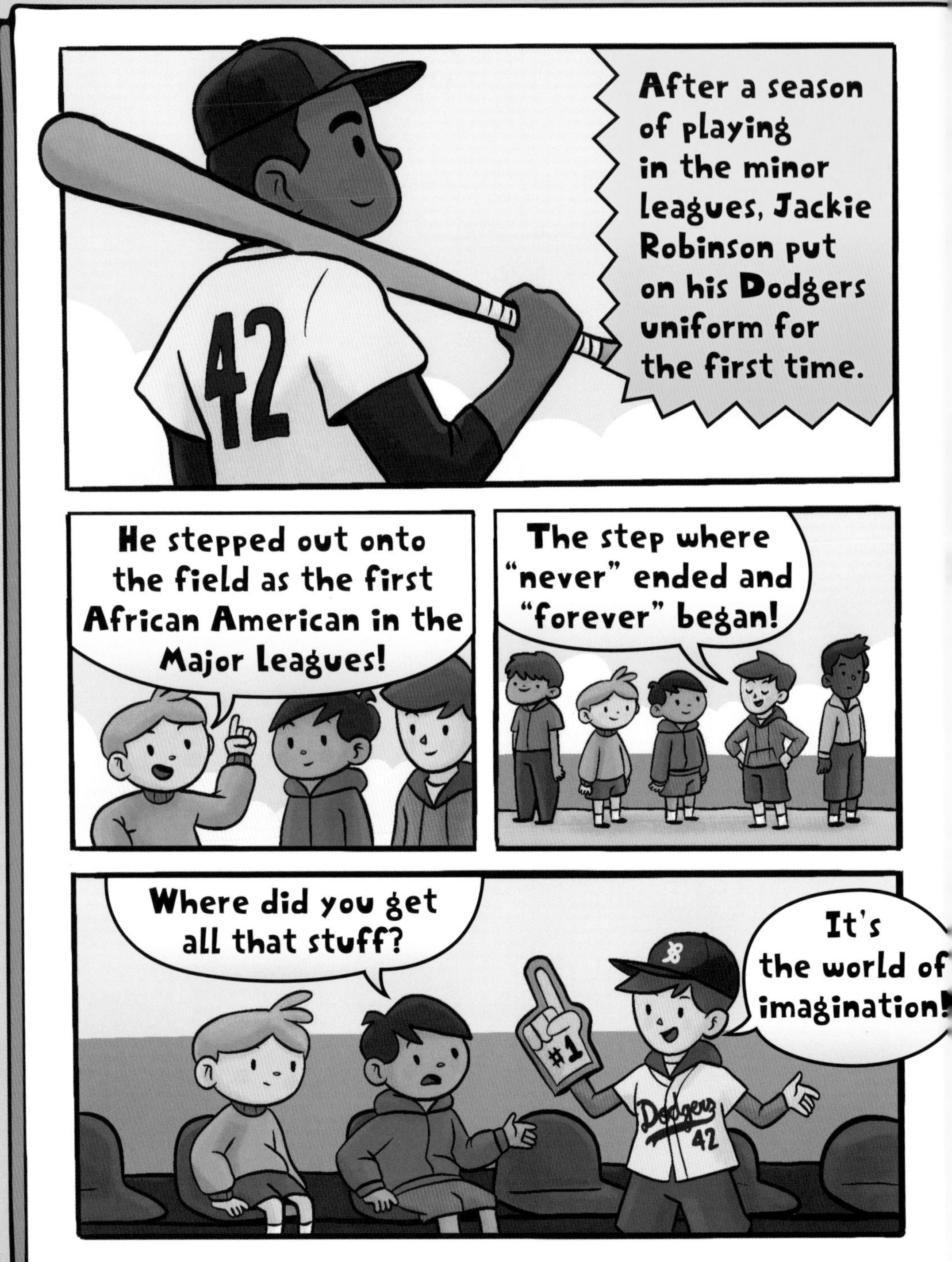

After a season of playing in the minor leagues, Jackie Robinson put on his Dodgers uniform for the first time.
42
He stepped out onto the field as the first African American in the Major Leagues!
The step where "never" ended and "forever" began!
Where did you get all that stuff?
It's the world of imagination!
#1
Dodgers
42

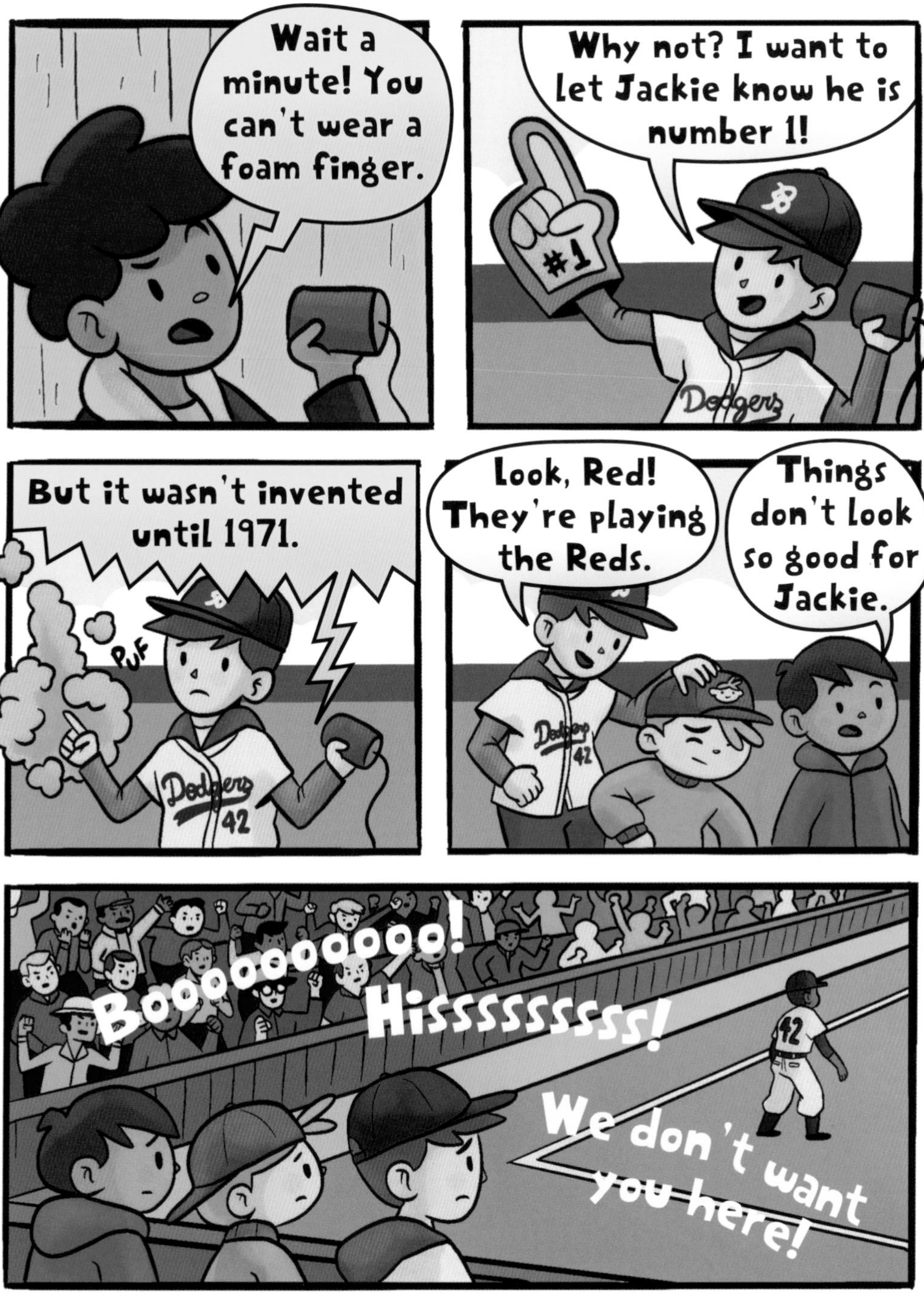
Wait a minute! You can't wear a foam finger.
Why not? I want to let Jackie know he is number 1!
#1
Dodgers
But it wasn't invented until 1971.
PUF
Dodgers
42
Look, Red! They're playing the Reds.
Things don't look so good for Jackie.
Dodgers
42
Boooooooooo!
Hisssssssss!
42
We don't want you here!

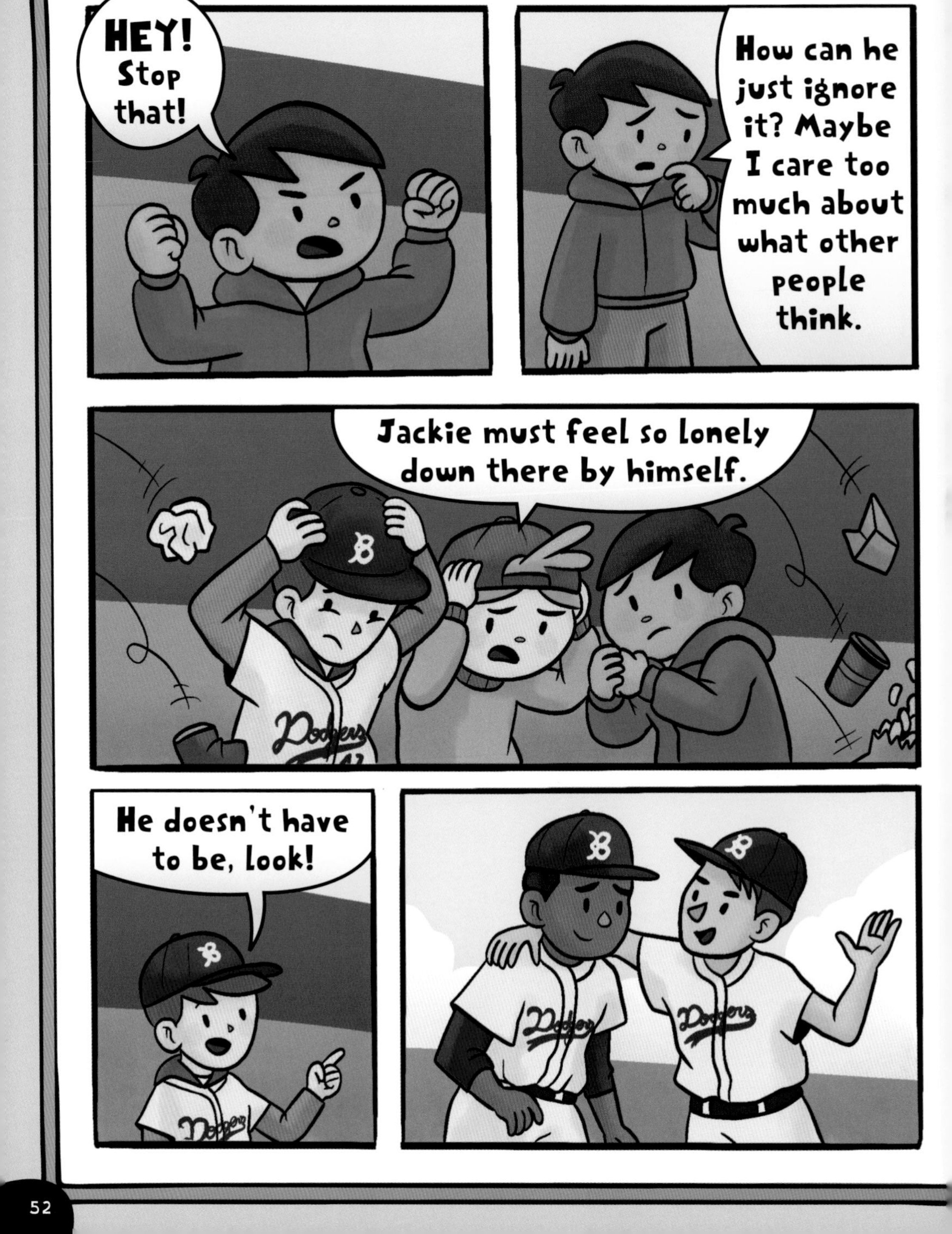
HEY! Stop that!
How can he just ignore it? Maybe I care too much about what other people think.
Jackie must feel so lonely down there by himself.
He doesn't have to be, look!

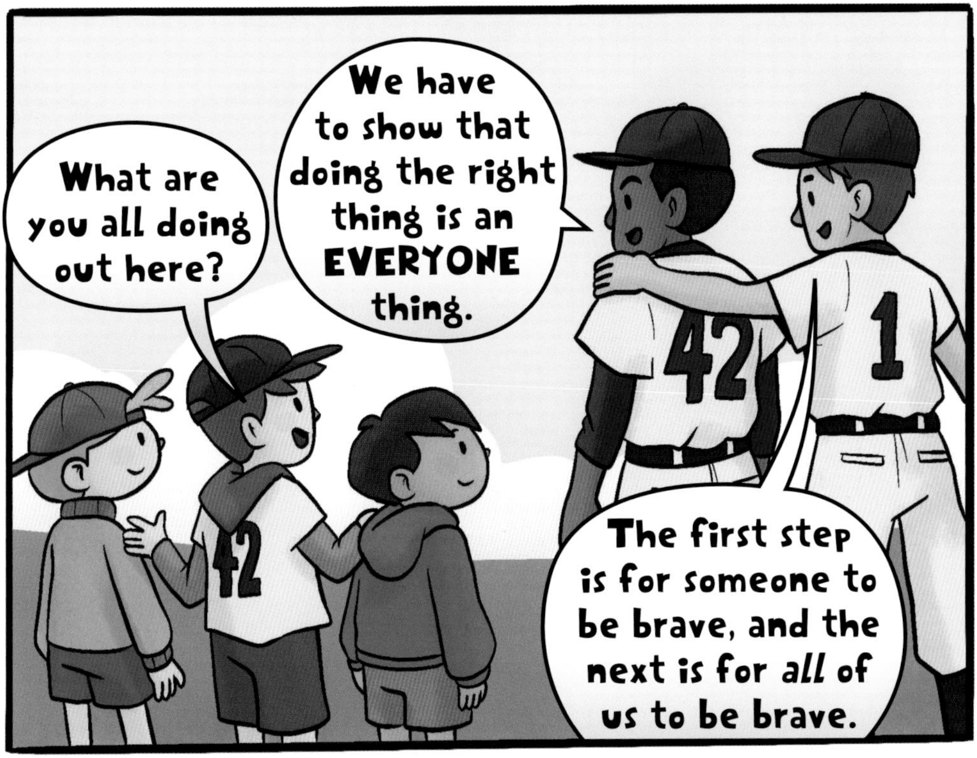
What are you all doing out here?
We have to show that doing the right thing is an EVERYONE thing.
The first step is for someone to be brave, and the next is for *all* of us to be brave.

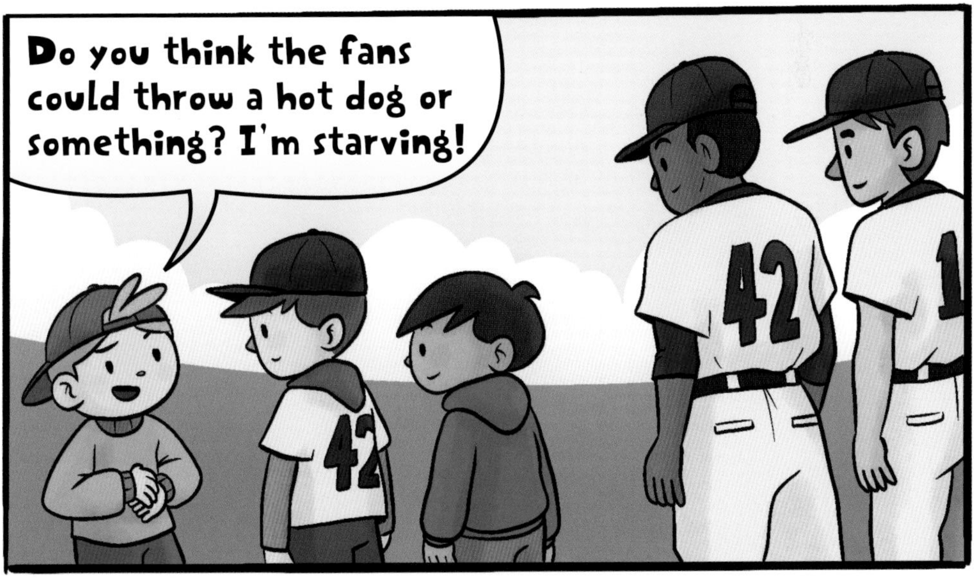
Do you think the fans could throw a hot dog or something? I'm starving!

CHAPTER SEVEN

Dodging Trolleys

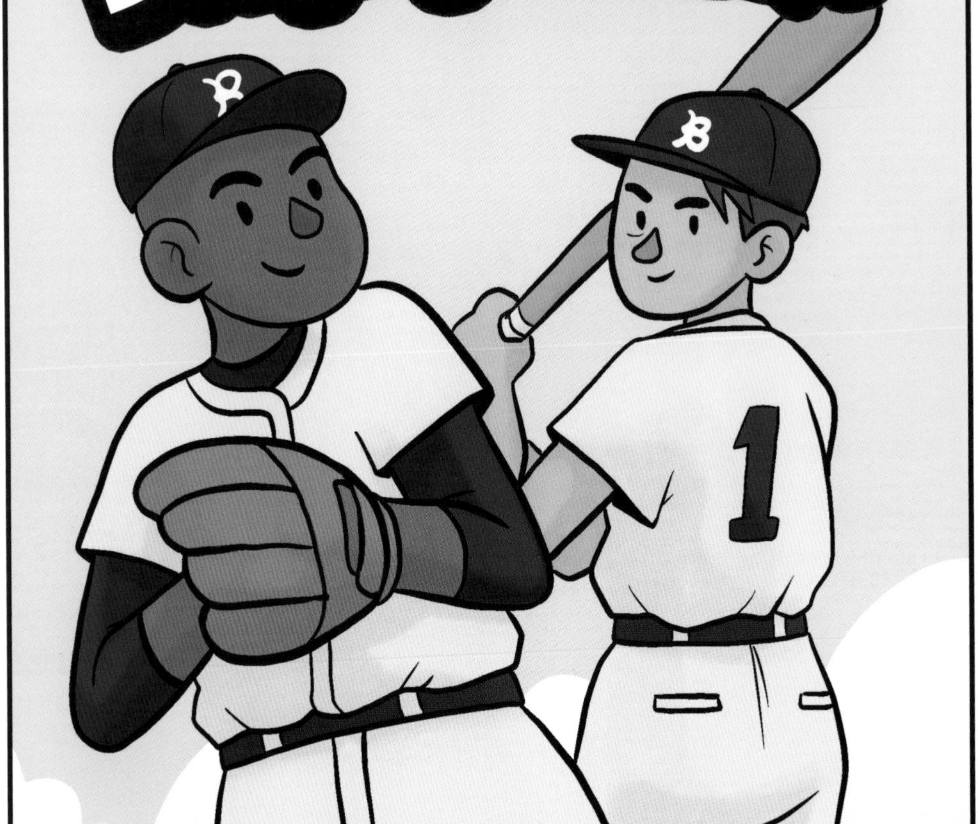

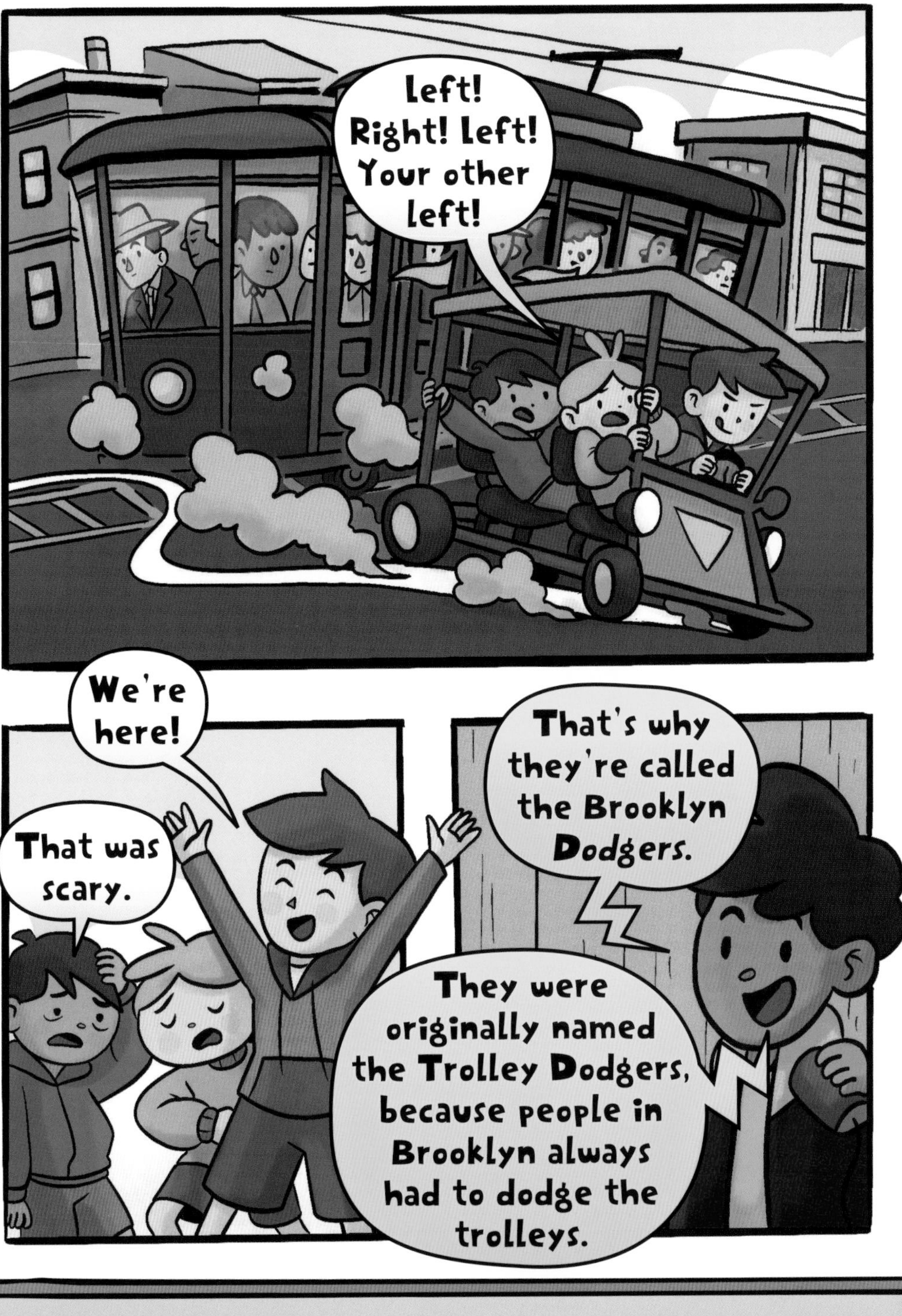
Left! Right! Left! Your other left!
We're here!
That was scary.
That's why they're called the Brooklyn Dodgers.
They were originally named the Trolley Dodgers, because people in Brooklyn always had to dodge the trolleys.

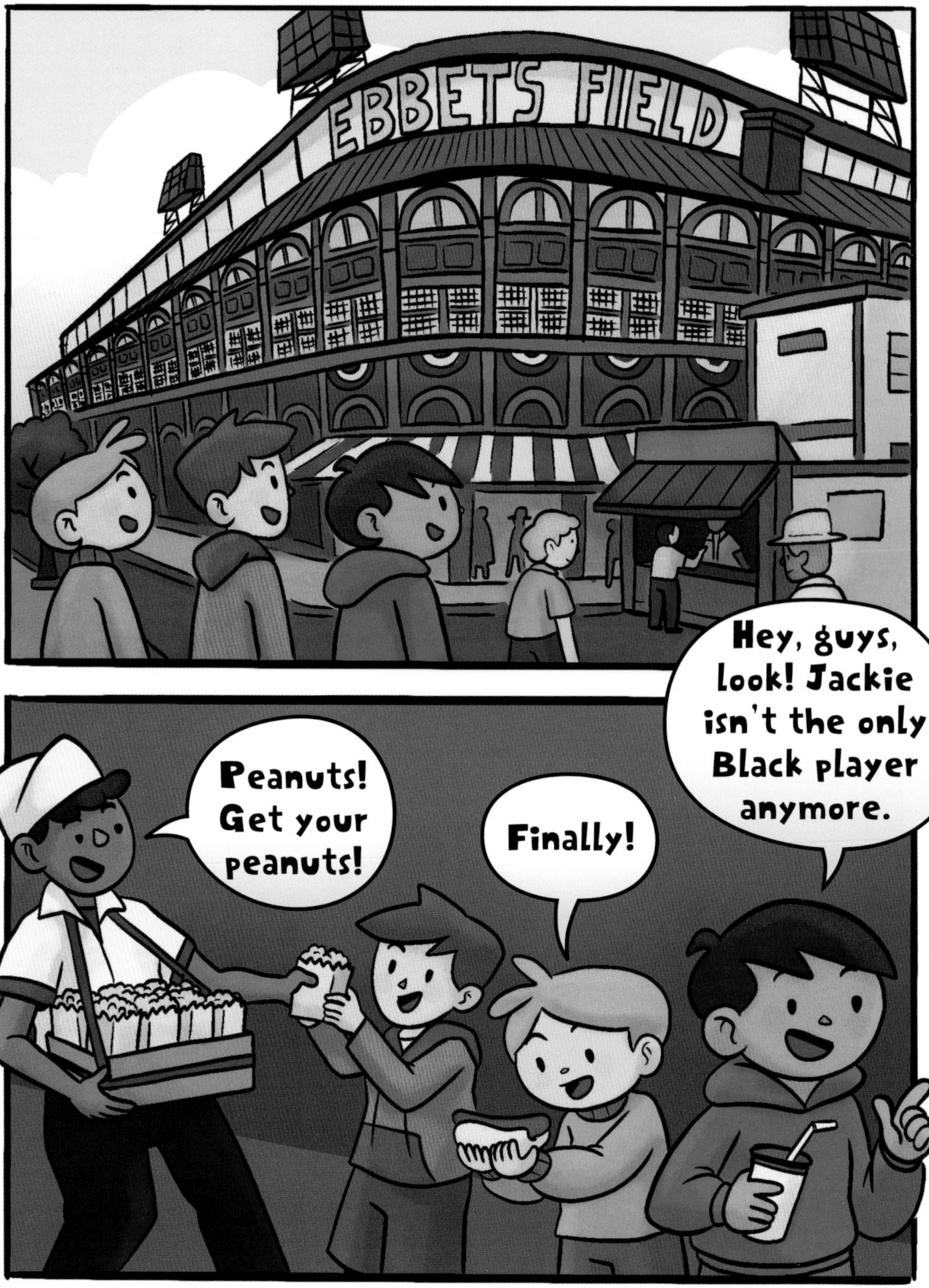
EBBETS FIELD
Peanuts! Get your peanuts!
Finally!
Hey, guys, look! Jackie isn't the only Black player anymore.

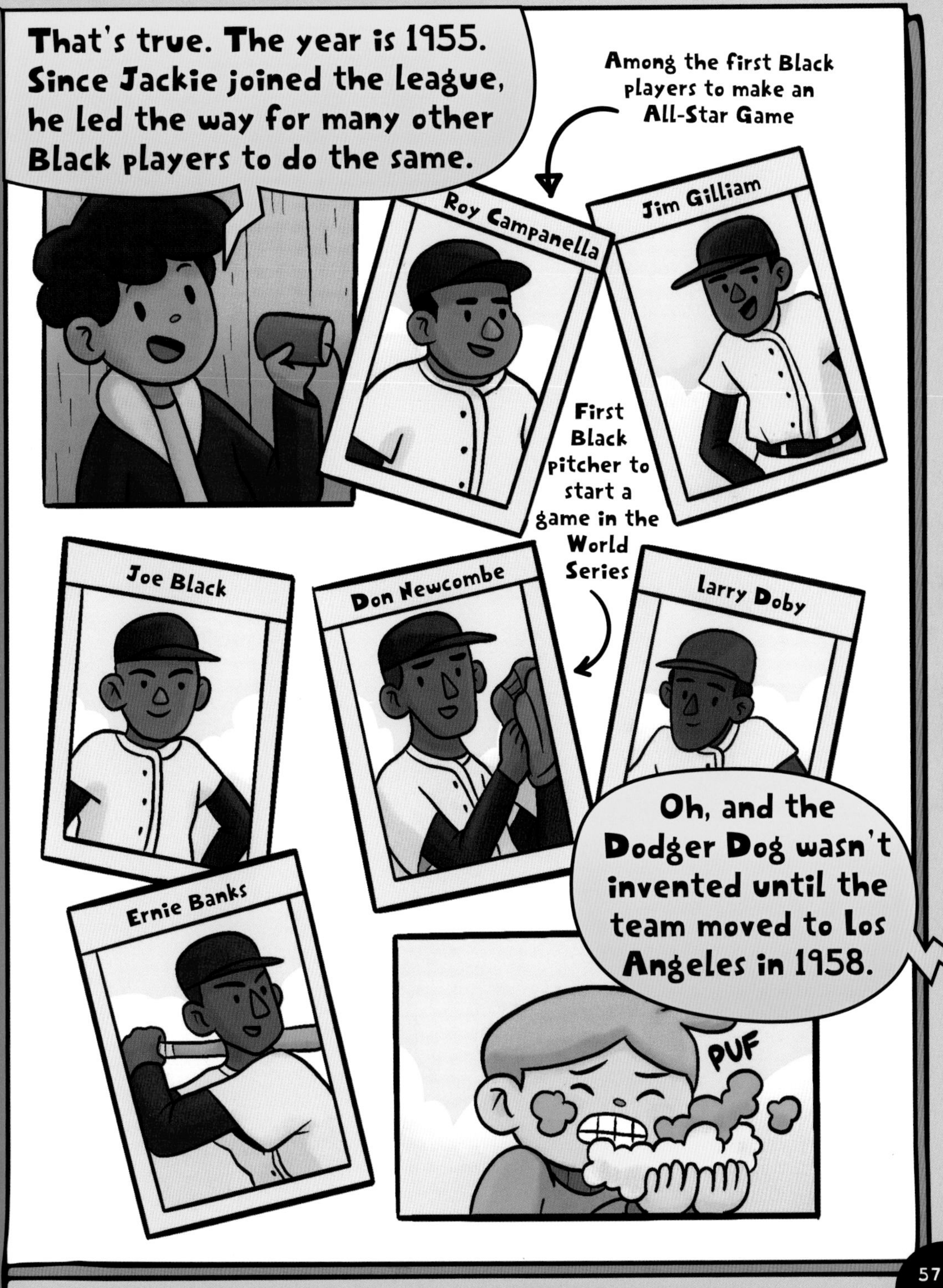
That's true. The year is 1955. Since Jackie joined the league, he led the way for many other Black players to do the same.
Among the first Black players to make an All-Star Game
Roy Campanella
Jim Gilliam
First Black pitcher to start a game in the World Series
Joe Black
Don Newcombe
Larry Doby
Ernie Banks
Oh, and the Dodger Dog wasn't invented until the team moved to Los Angeles in 1958.
PUF

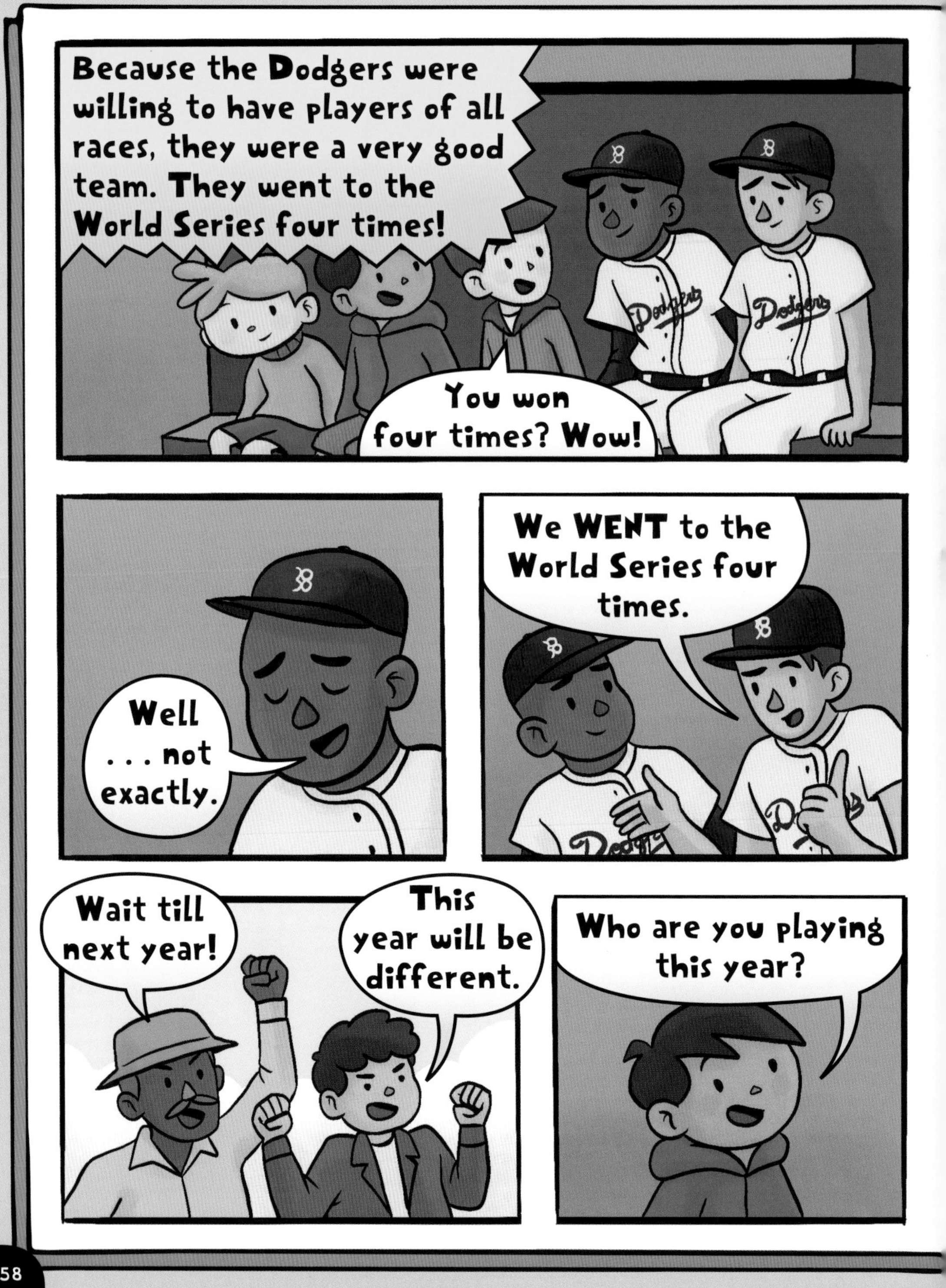
Because the Dodgers were willing to have players of all races, they were a very good team. They went to the World Series four times!
You won four times? Wow!
Well . . . not exactly.
We WENT to the World Series four times.
Wait till next year!
This year will be different.
Who are you playing this year?

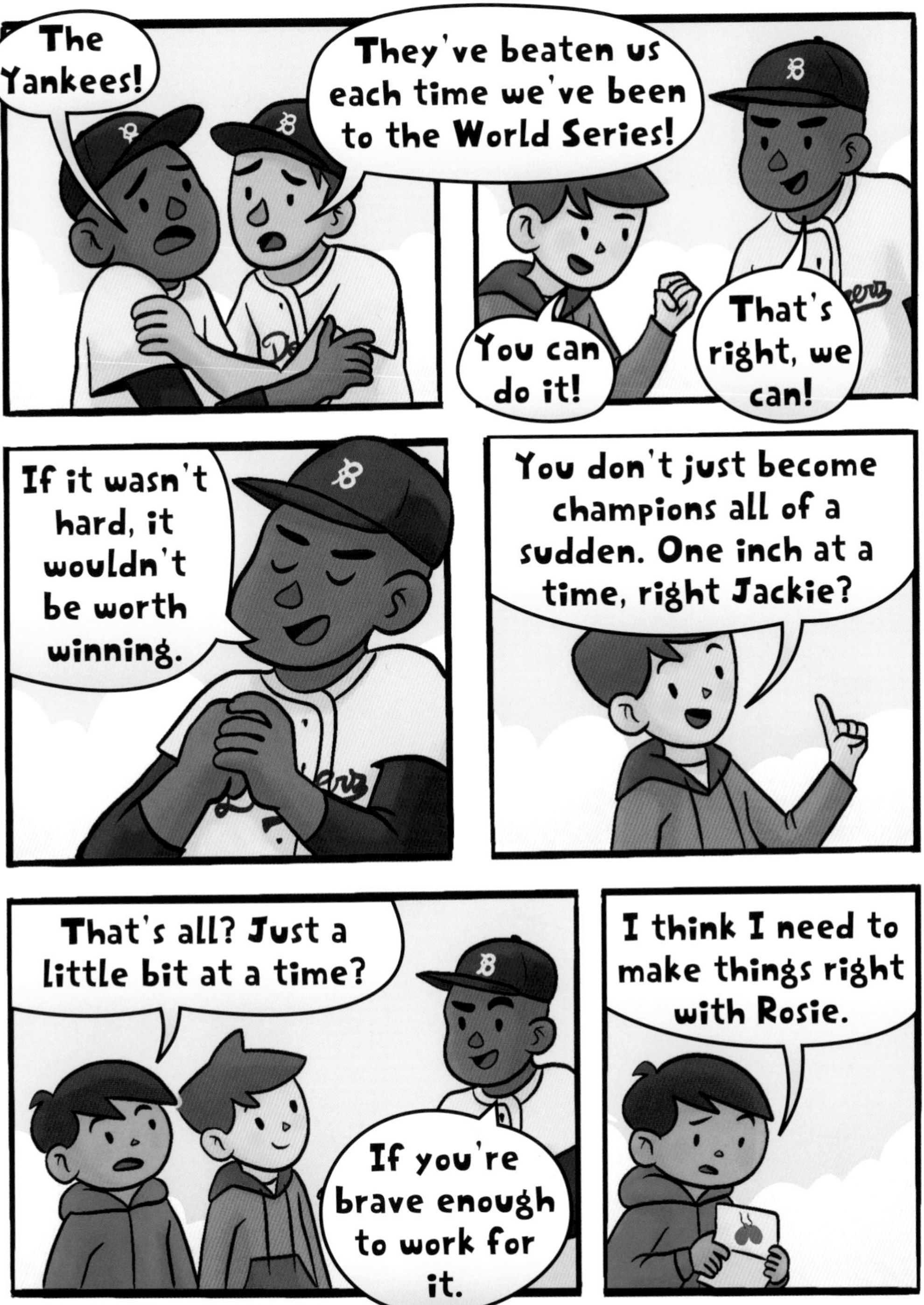
The Yankees!
They've beaten us each time we've been to the World Series!
You can do it!
That's right, we can!
If it wasn't hard, it wouldn't be worth winning.
You don't just become champions all of a sudden. One inch at a time, right Jackie?
That's all? Just a little bit at a time?
If you're brave enough to work for it.
I think I need to make things right with Rosie.

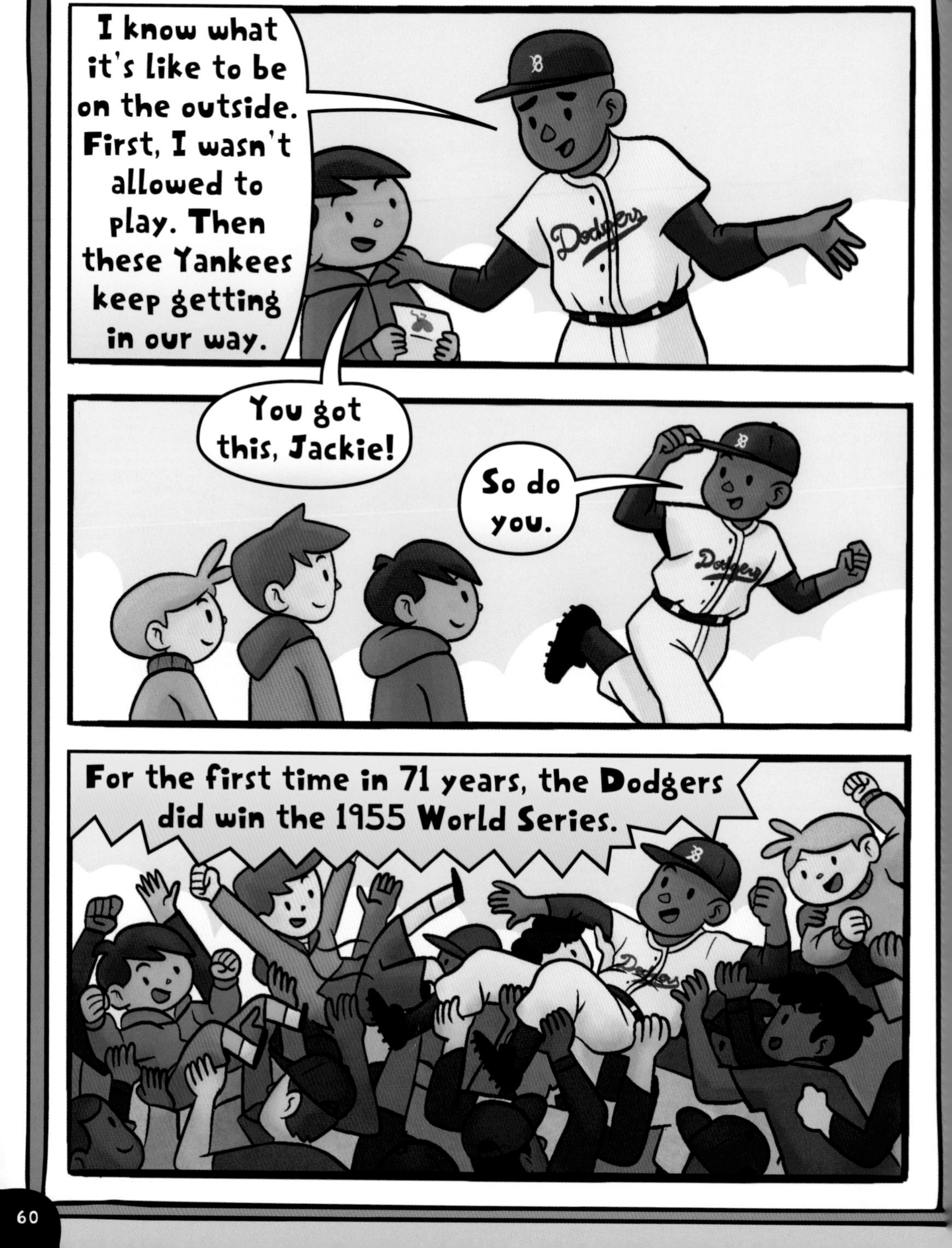
I know what it's like to be on the outside. First, I wasn't allowed to play. Then these Yankees keep getting in our way.
You got this, Jackie!
So do you.
For the first time in 71 years, the Dodgers did win the 1955 World Series.

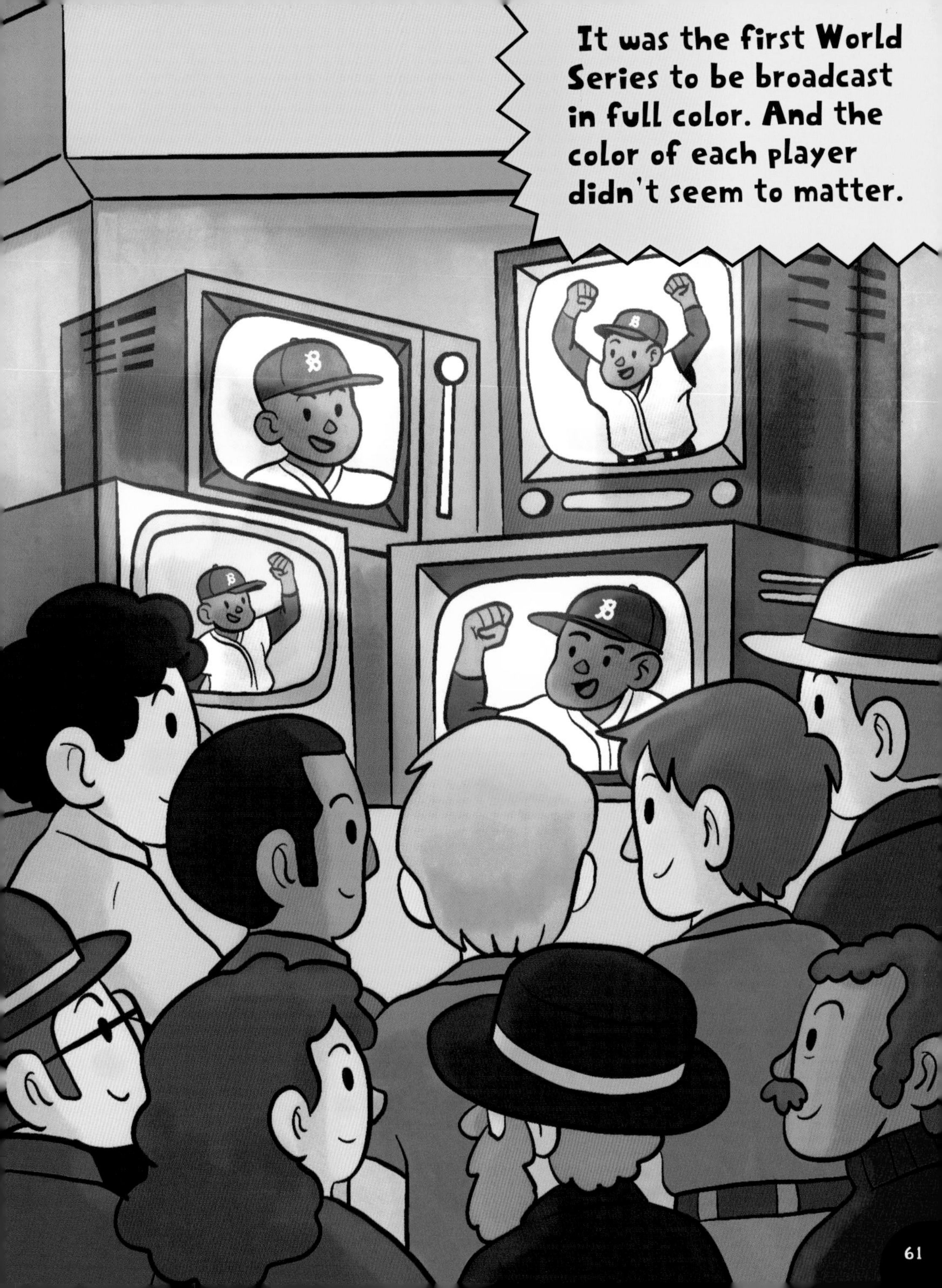
It was the first World Series to be broadcast in full color. And the color of each player didn't seem to matter.

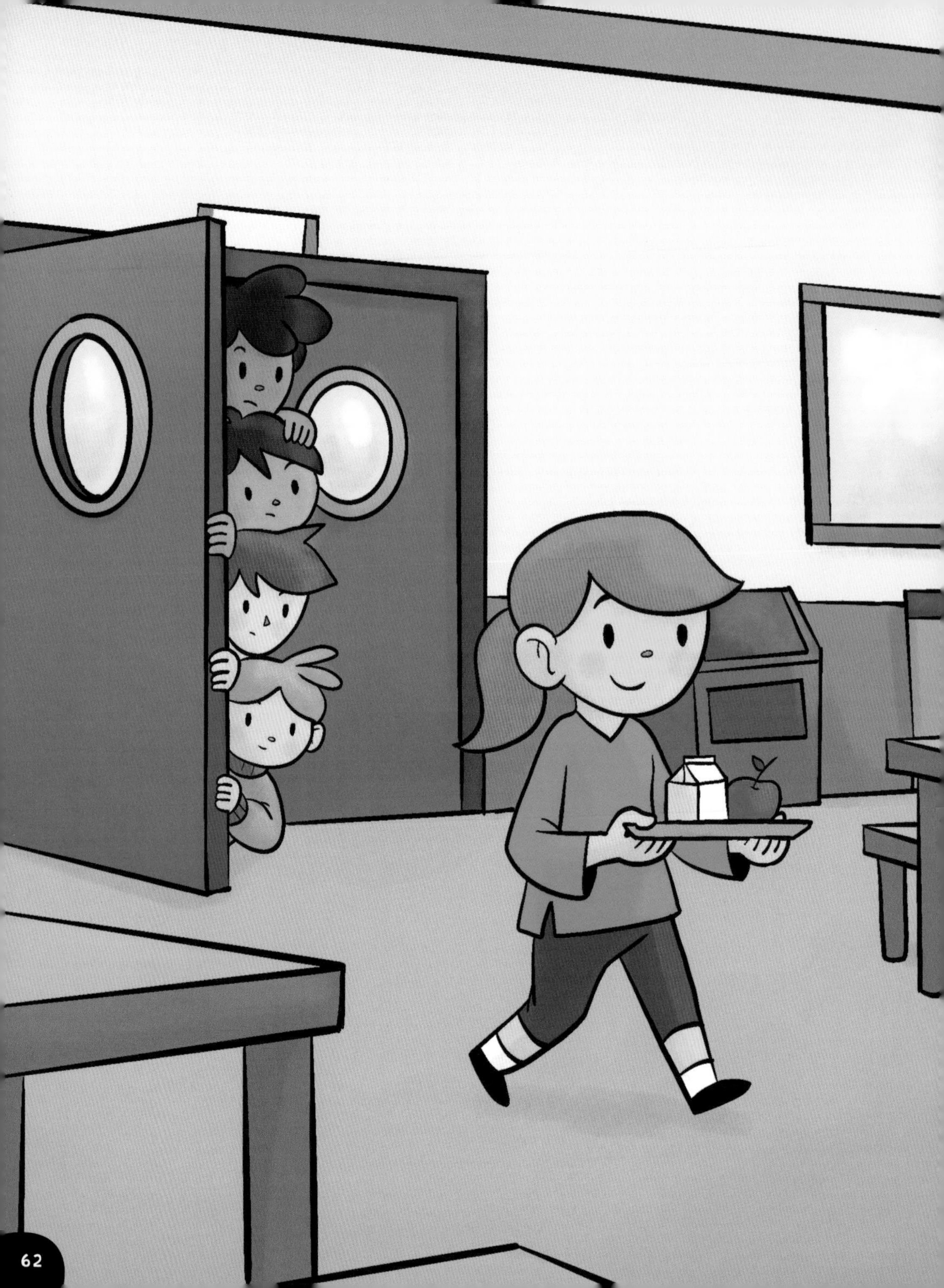

CHAPTER EIGHT

Rosie and the Dufus

With sweaty palms, Marty tightly held the invitation in his hands. Like international spies, the boys peered through the window to find Rosie in the cafeteria.

I can't believe I'm going to do this. I must be crazy.

Lucky grabbed Marty by the shoulders. "Is Rosie your best friend?"

"She's the best." Marty knew what he had to do, what he *wanted* to do, but he was still nervous to do it.

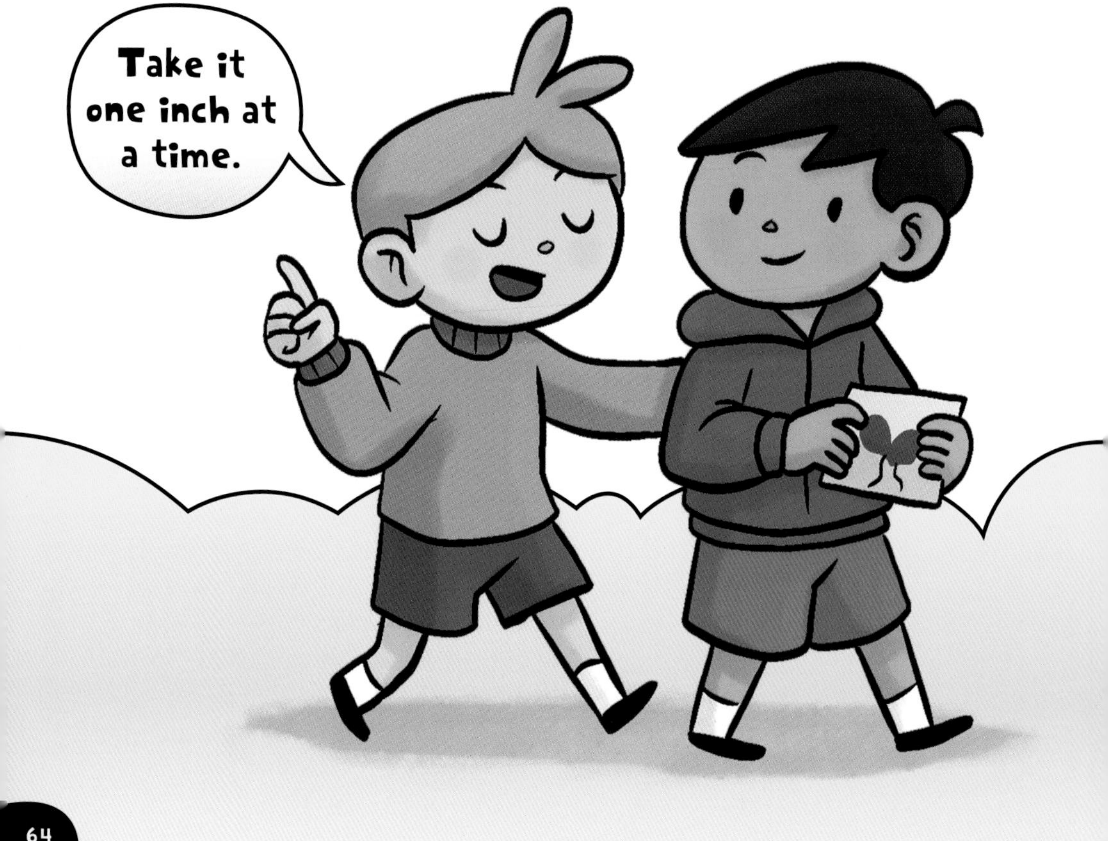
Take it one inch at a time.

"Besides, you can't do the right thing without *trying* to do the right thing." Lucky pushed Marty into the cafeteria.

"B-B-But I'm scared. What if the guys make fun of me?"

"Maybe they aren't brave enough yet to be friends with girls or to do the right thing. Maybe they need you to be brave first and lead the way," Lucky said.

Marty gulped. He started walking slowly but gained speed like a brave locomotive. He walked right up to Rosie in the middle of the cafeteria:

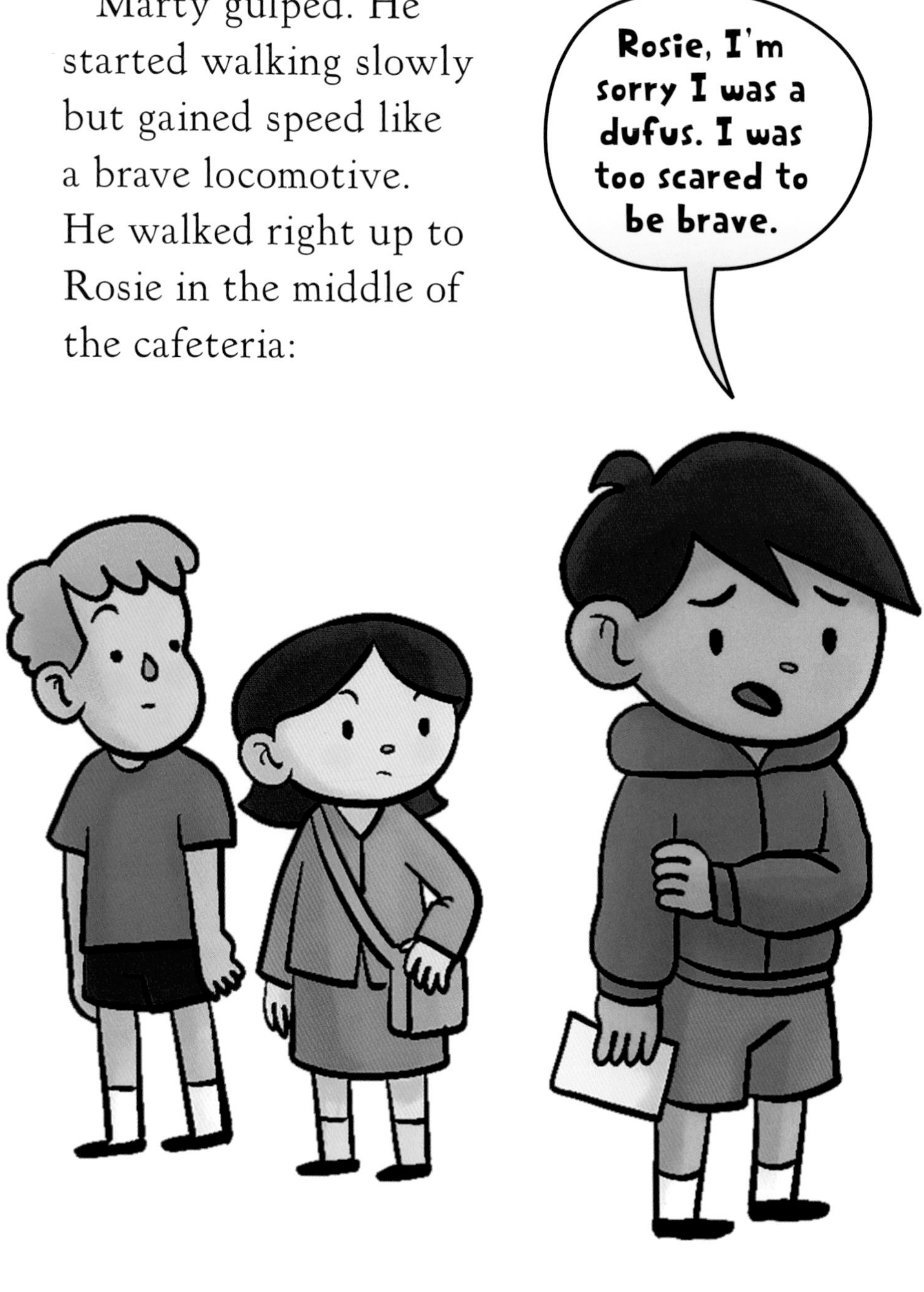
Rosie, I'm sorry I was a dufus. I was too scared to be brave.

The entire room stood in shocked silence. Marty could feel hundreds of eyes staring at him. He took a deep breath—then climbed right on top of the table!

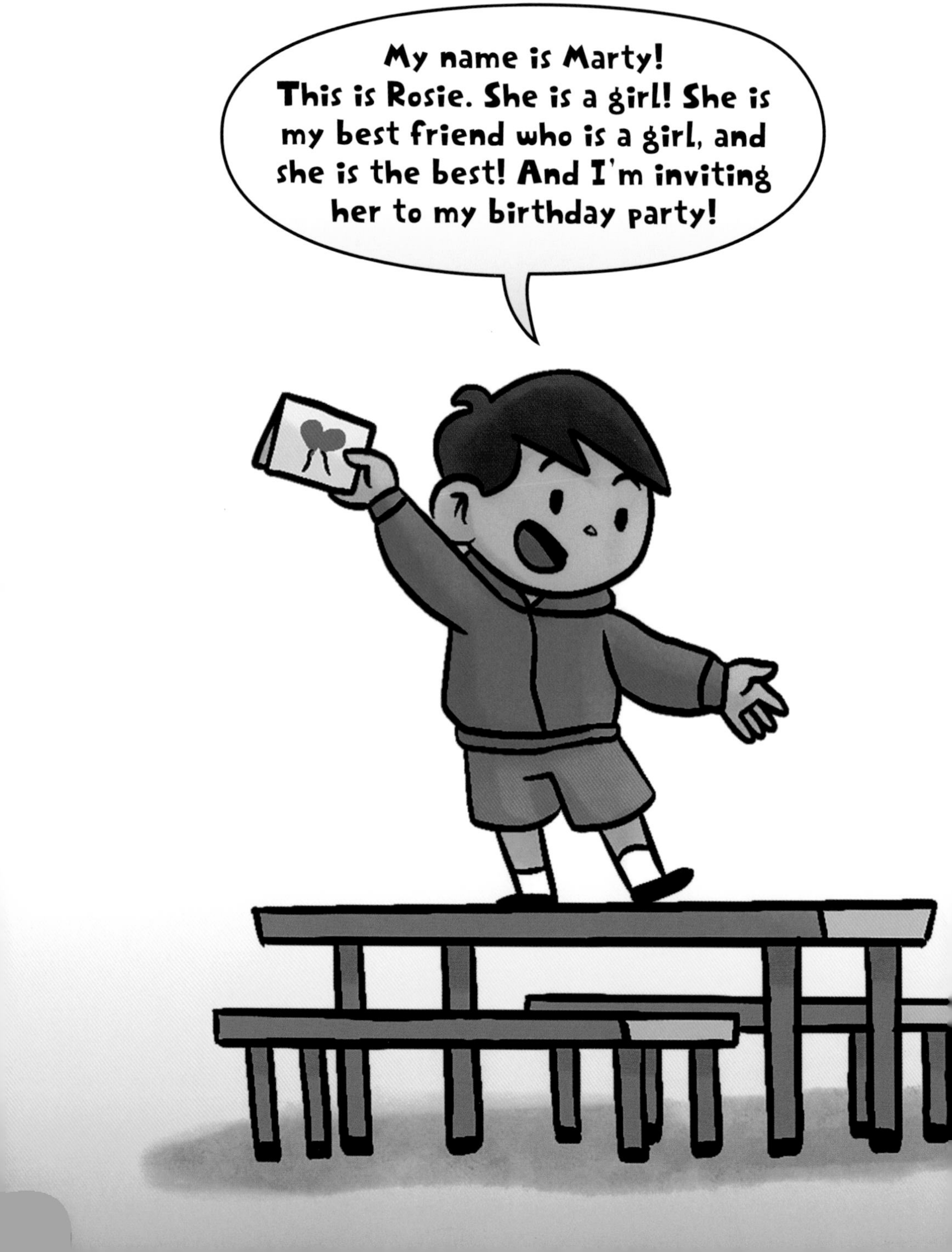
My name is Marty! This is Rosie. She is a girl! She is my best friend who is a girl, and she is the best! And I'm inviting her to my birthday party!

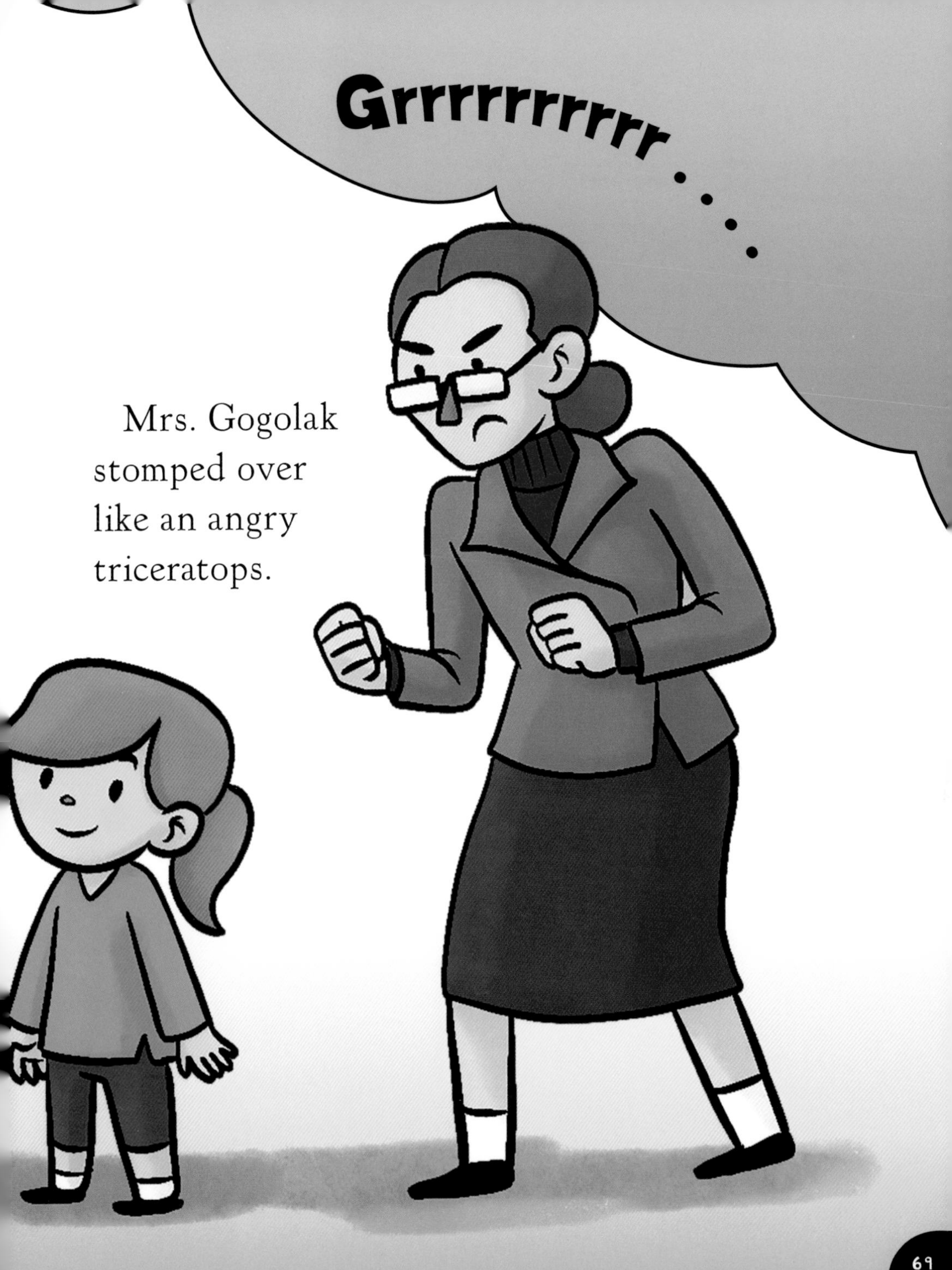
Grrrrrrrrrr....

Mrs. Gogolak stomped over like an angry triceratops.

Rosie grabbed Marty by the hand and yanked him down just in time. "I know I'm your best friend. I just wanted you to be brave enough to stand up to those boys."

"You are pretty smart, huh?" Marty blushed.

"Well, I *am* the best," Rosie said. She slugged Marty in the arm.

The two of them were suddenly engulfed by a dark, ominous shadow.

Marty? You're going to be friends with . . . a girl?

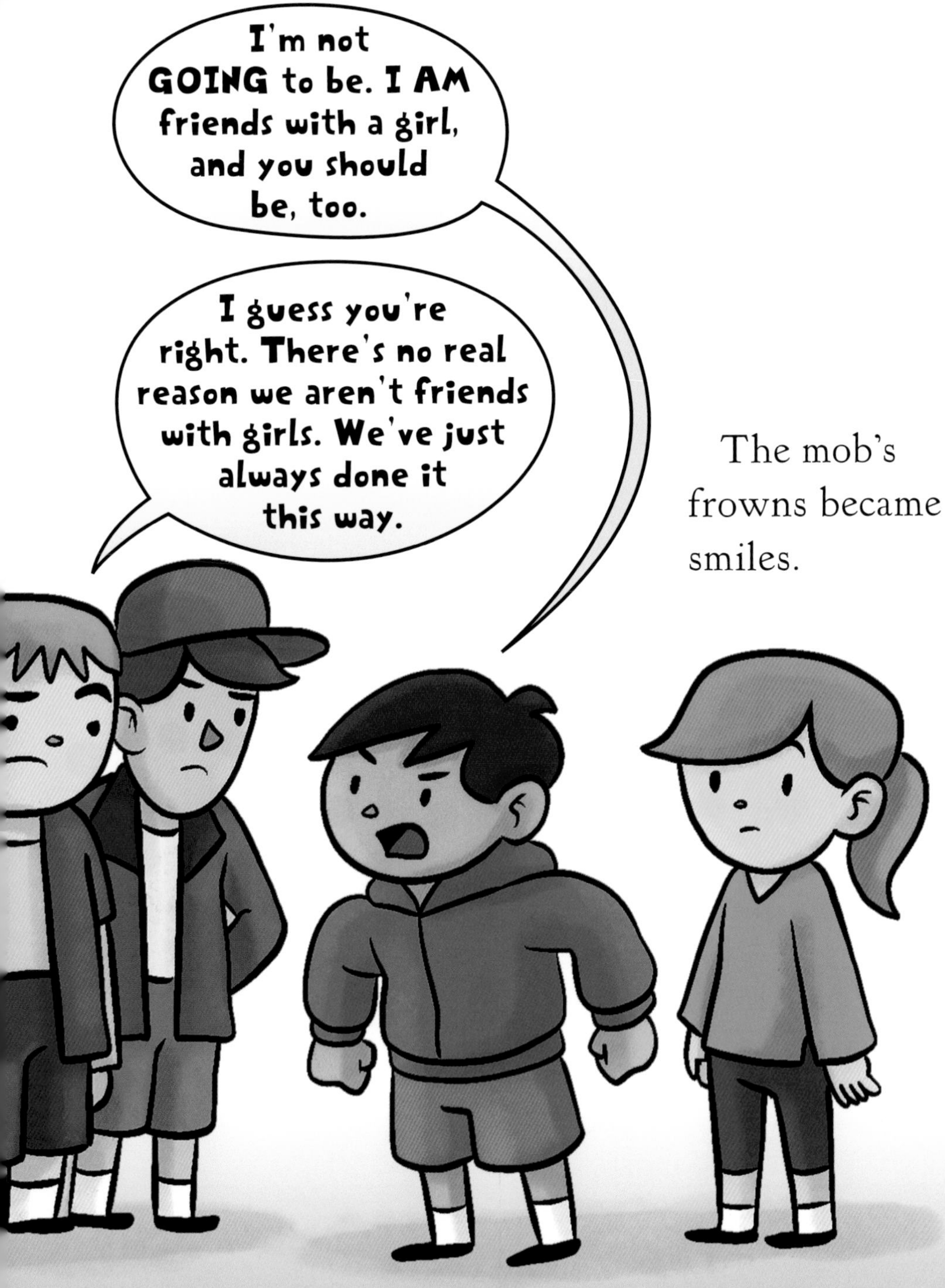
I'm not GOING to be. I AM friends with a girl, and you should be, too.
I guess you're right. There's no real reason we aren't friends with girls. We've just always done it this way.

The mob's frowns became smiles.

"The step where 'never' ended and 'forever' began!" Lucky cheered. "Another big win for the Good Guys Agency, and another successful chapter for The Book of the Future. Did we get all of that down?"

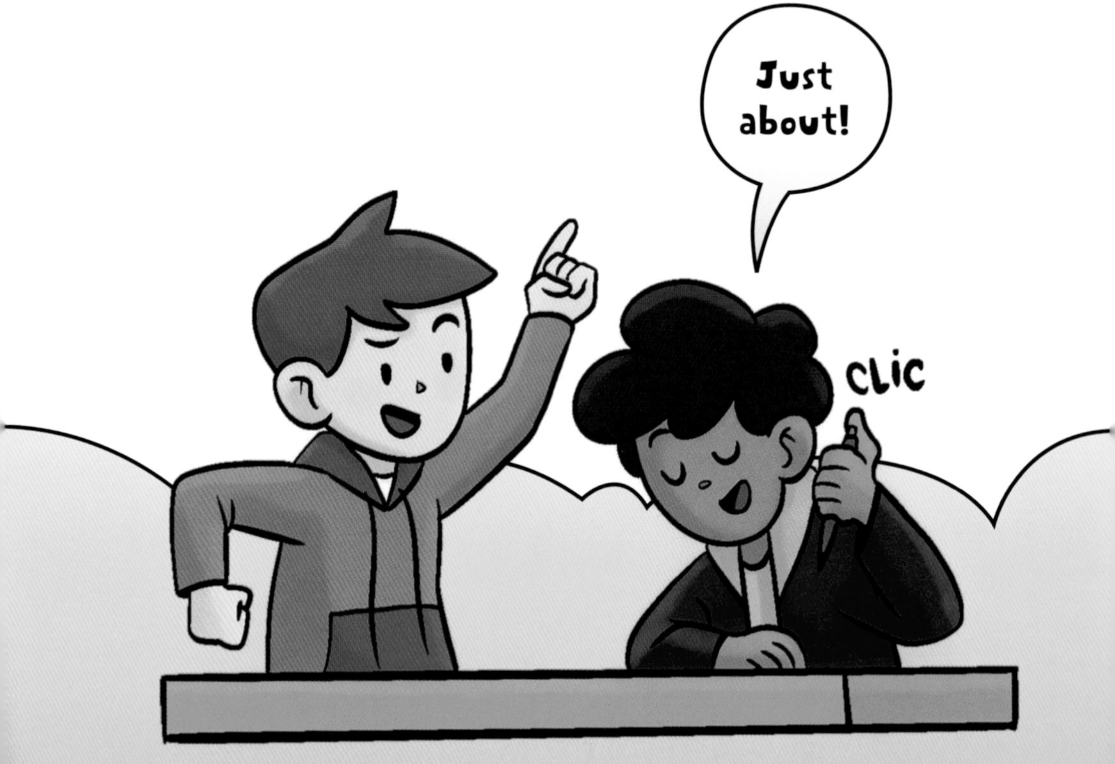
Just about!
CLIC

"Come on, fellas, back to base!"
Lucky took a right to exit the building.

But we still have class!

"Oh, right." Lucky turned around, dragging his backpack behind him.

CHAPTER NINE

The One Thing

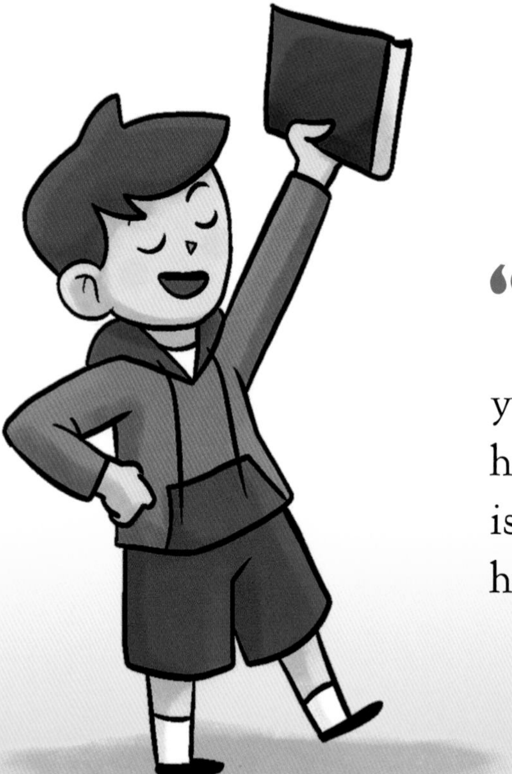

"Ah! Rudy, you outdid yourself." Lucky held the latest issue over his head in triumph.

"Ya know, fellas, Jackie made me think about The Book of the Future a little differently," Rudy said.

"What do you mean?" Red asked.

Jackie taught us that doing the right thing happens a little at a time. So maybe changing the world doesn't happen in the future; maybe it happens right now.

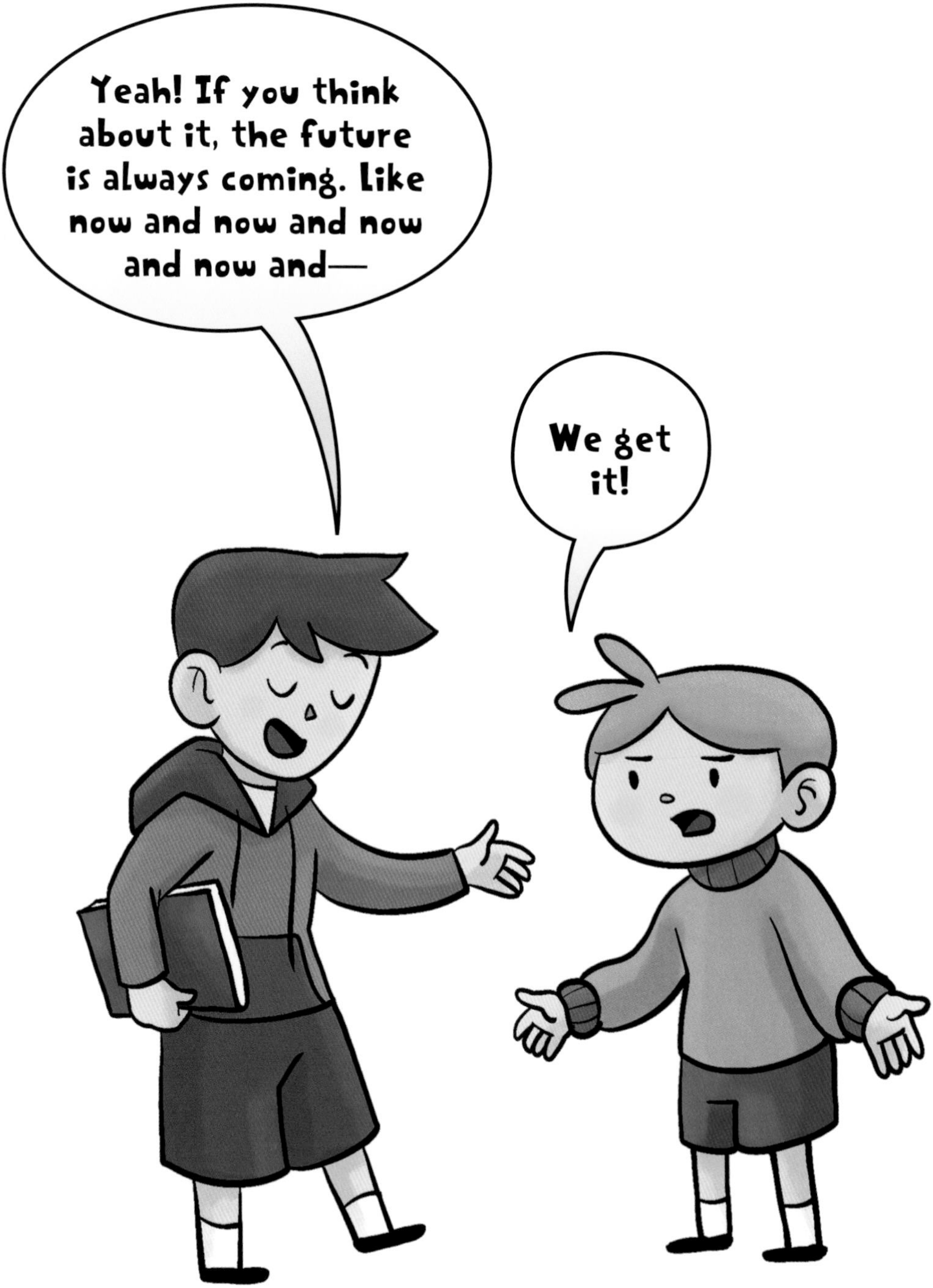
Yeah! If you think about it, the future is always coming. Like now and now and now and now and—
We get it!

We don't grow up all in one day. We grow up a little every day. And every day, there are scary things to face. Being brave is something that we have to practice.

"Okay," Lucky said, "but except for tropical birds! They give me the willies." he shivered.

"Wait! You're afraid of tropical birds?" Red and Rudy exploded with laughter.

Lucky shrugged with embarrassment.

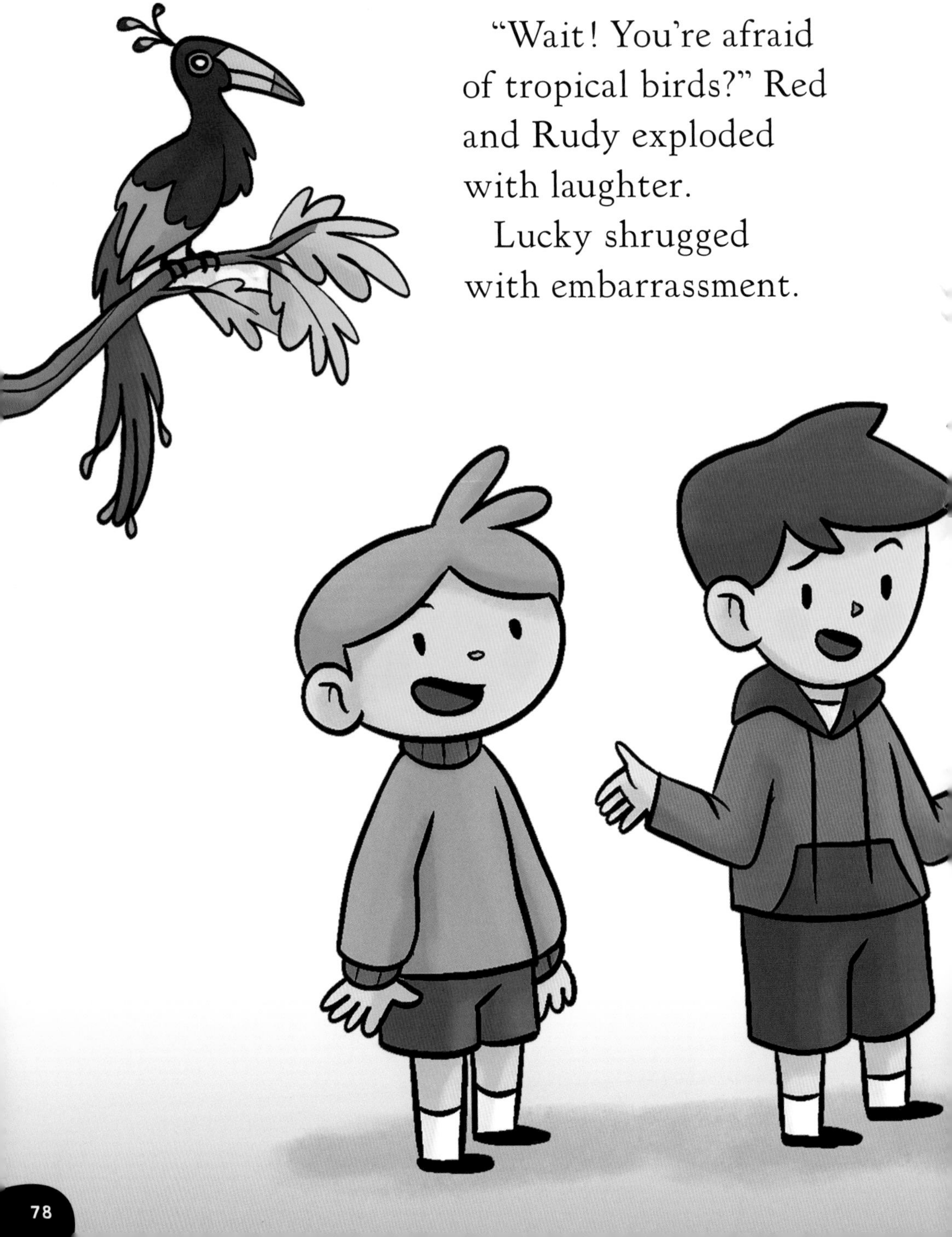

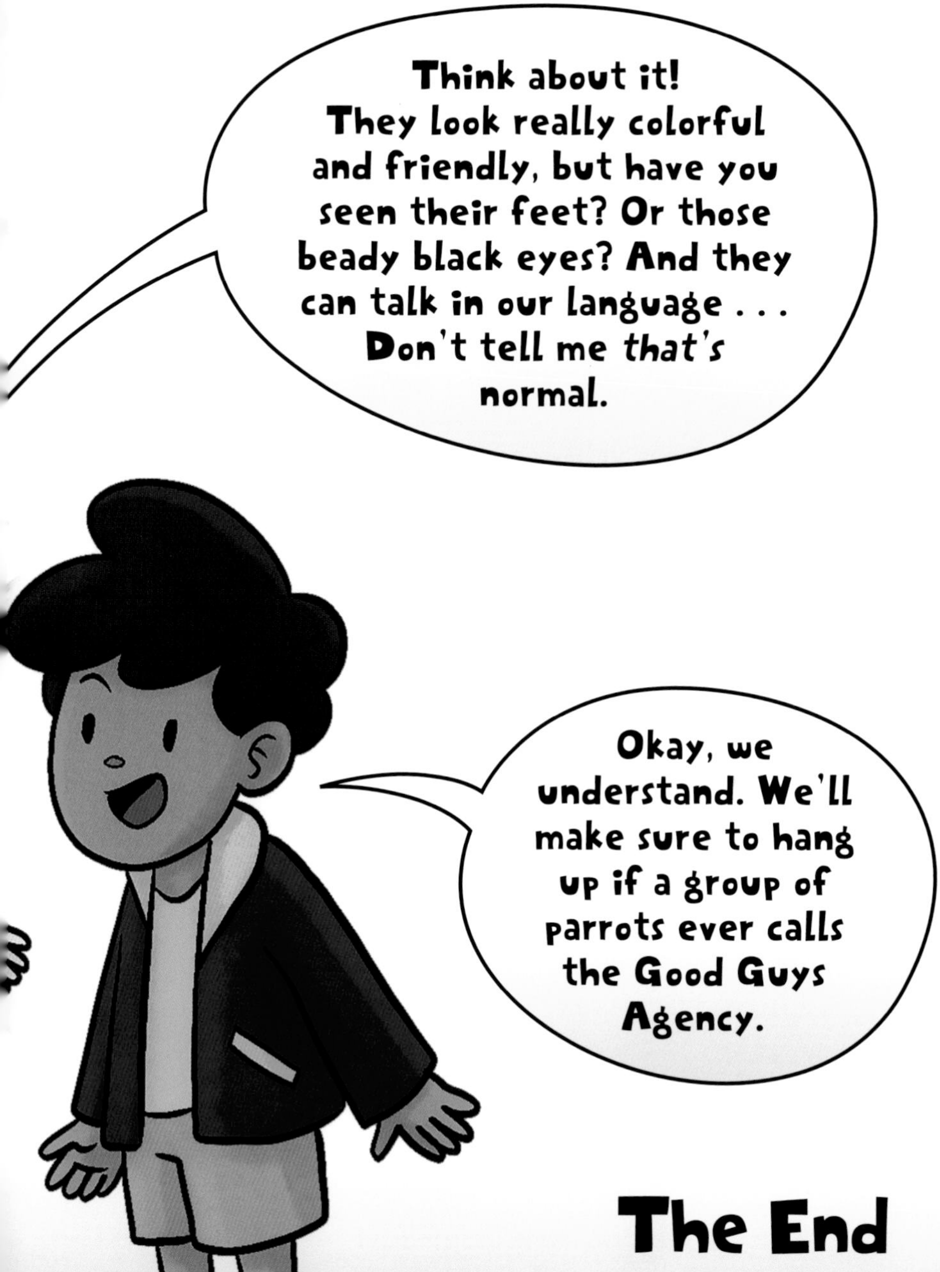
Think about it! They look really colorful and friendly, but have you seen their feet? Or those beady black eyes? And they can talk in our language . . . Don't tell me *that's* normal.
Okay, we understand. We'll make sure to hang up if a group of parrots ever calls the Good Guys Agency.
The End

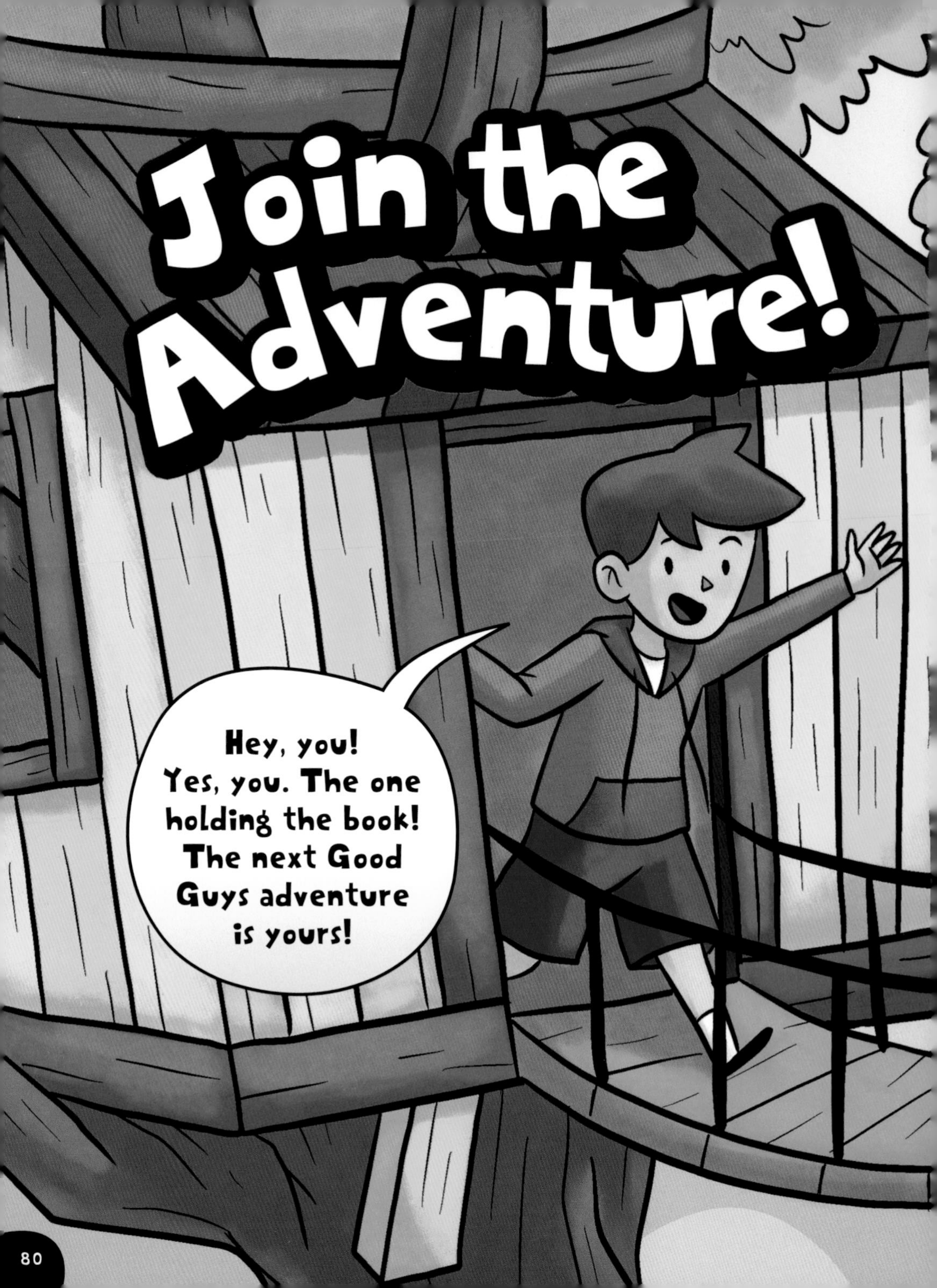
Join the Adventure!
Hey, you! Yes, you. The one holding the book! The next Good Guys adventure is yours!

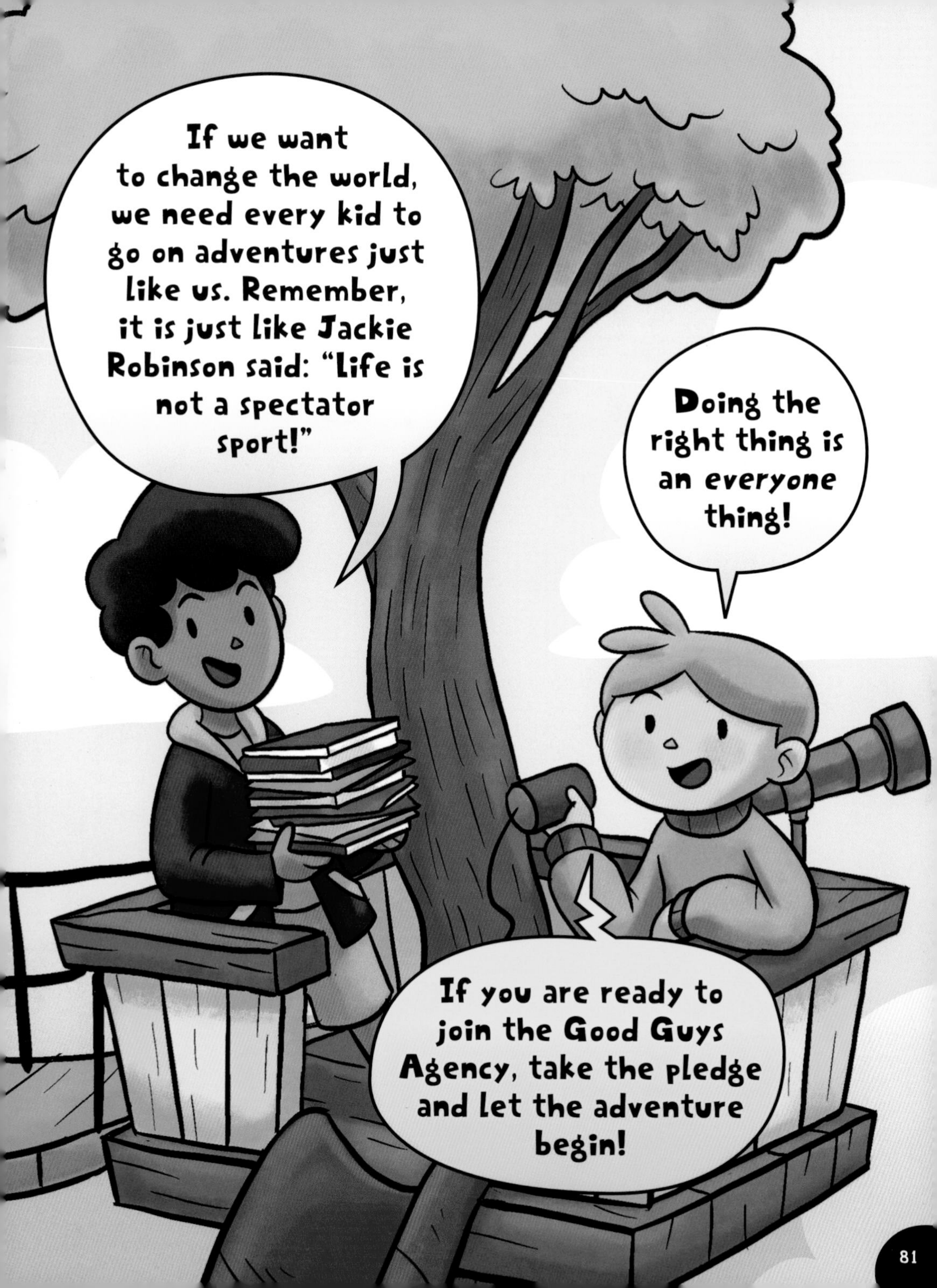
If we want to change the world, we need every kid to go on adventures just like us. Remember, it is just like Jackie Robinson said: "Life is not a spectator sport!"
Doing the right thing is an *everyone* thing!
If you are ready to join the Good Guys Agency, take the pledge and let the adventure begin!

We Pledge to:

Be Kind to Others
Speak Nicely
Creatively Solve Problems
Treat Everyone with Respect
Include Others
Work Together
Love Others for Who They Are
Try New Things
Think before Reacting
Tell the Truth
Ask Questions

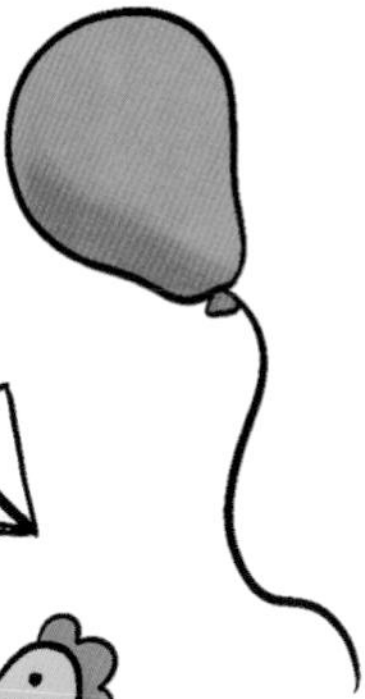
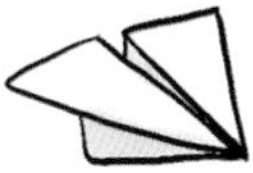
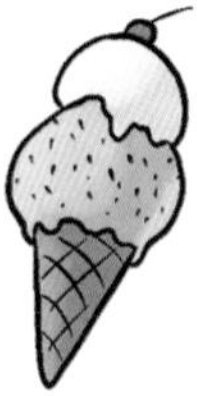
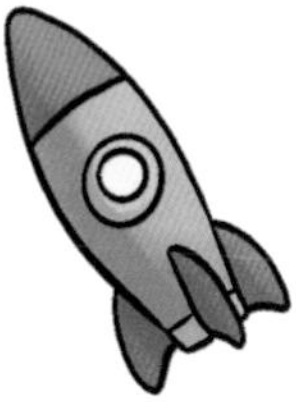
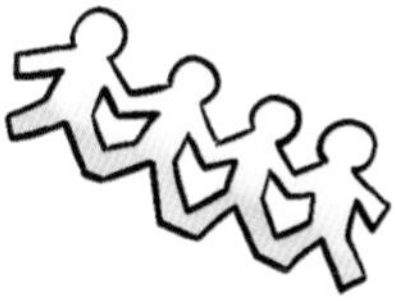
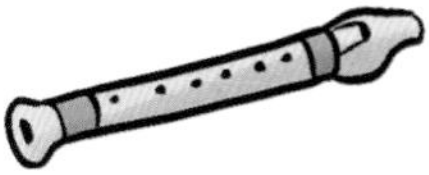
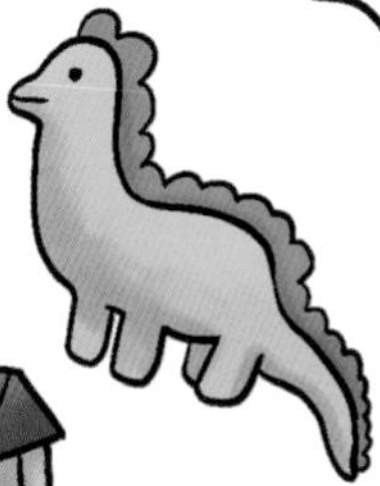
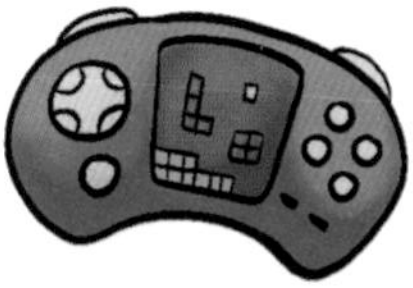
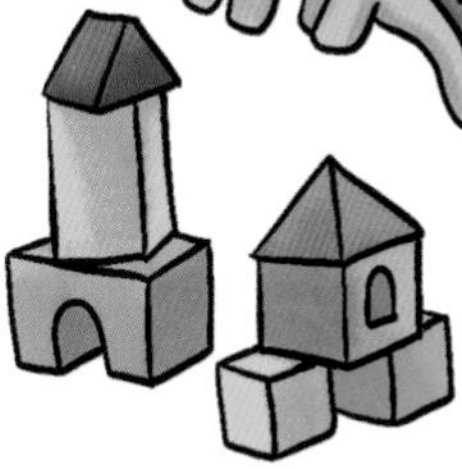
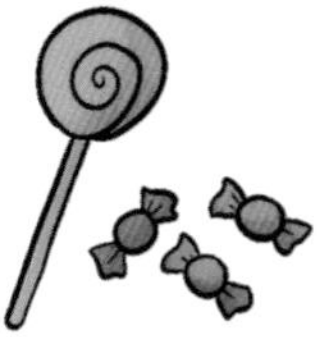
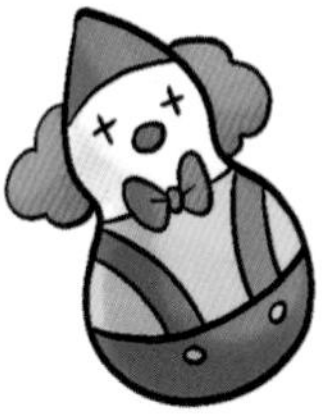
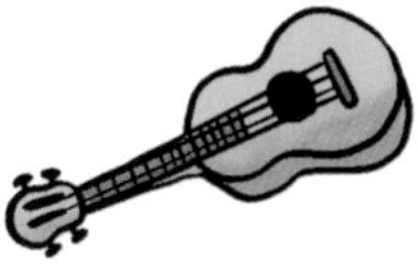

Be Positive
Always Be Learning
Take Care of Others
Apply Ourselves
Be Patient
Smile Big
Dance Goofy
Imagine for Fun

The future is now;
there is no need to wait.
Use it to help others, and
good will become great.

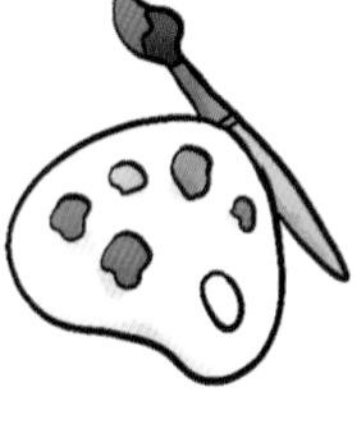
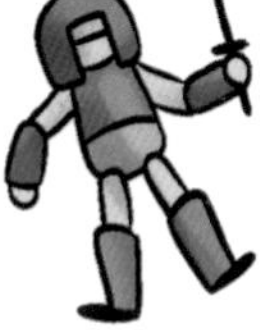
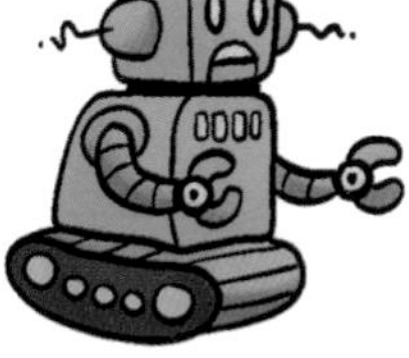
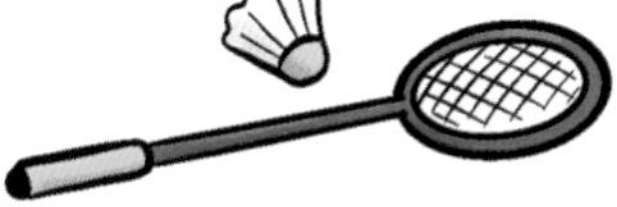
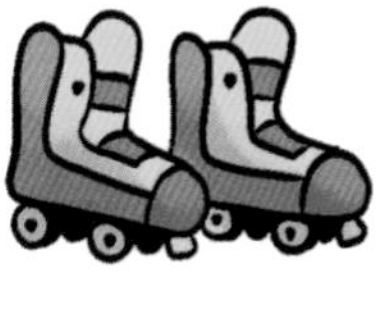

All About Jackie Robinson

Jackie Robinson was born in Cairo, Georgia, in 1919. Jackie had four siblings and was raised by his mother. His family grew up in Pasadena, California, in a neighborhood that was predominantly white. The prejudice that they faced prepared Jackie for his courageous career as the first Major League Baseball player to break the color barrier.

From a young age, Jackie was a tremendous athlete. He went to college at UCLA, where he earned varsity letters in four different sports (the first athlete to ever do it!). Robinson had to leave college early because of financial hardships and joined the United States Army instead. He got into trouble (he was court-martialed) when he stood up to incidents of racial discrimination, and he had to leave the army.

Jackie then became a professional baseball player. He started playing for the Kansas City Monarchs of the Negro Leagues. His success drew the eye of Brooklyn Dodgers president Branch Rickey. In 1947, Rickey signed Jackie Robinson to join the Dodgers. During his time as a baseball player, he faced hatred and adversity. By the time he retired, he was the Rookie of the Year, an All-Star, a World Series Champion, and a Hall of Famer. But most importantly, he was a trailblazer and a civil rights activist who inspired future generations to do better.

Jackie while playing in Kansas City for the Negro leagues.

Jackie—number 42!—poses for a photograph in his Brooklyn Dodgers uniform.

About the Author

Nick Esposito is an award-winning teacher and education consultant with a passion for bringing best practices of service learning into the classroom. Nick has traveled around the world serving with different organizations for different cultures and peoples, from which he has developed the belief that educational experiences must sharpen the mind and embrace the heart. Nick has degrees from Villanova University (Journalism, Sociology, Peace & Justice), Johns Hopkins (Master's in Urban Education), and the University of Pennsylvania (Master's in Education Entrepreneurship). Nick is the ecstatic husband of the love of his life and "Habitat Crush," Cynthia. He is also a longtime hockey player and Philadelphia sports fan. He is the proud teacher of hundreds of students, all of whom are impacting the world in their own exciting, unique, yet quirky ways.

About the Illustrator

Ricardo Tokumoto was born in Limeira, Brazil. He moved to Belo Horizonte and attended the Faculty of Fine Arts at UFMG, where he graduated with a BA in Animation Cinema. Today, he works on webcomics, creates comics for authors and publishers, and also works as an illustrator and animator.

About Bushel & Peck Books

Bushel & Peck Books is a children's publishing house with a special mission. Through our Book-for-Book Promise™, we donate one book to kids in need for every book we sell. Our beautiful books are given to kids through schools, libraries, local neighborhoods, shelters, nonprofits, and also to many selfless organizations that are working hard to make a difference. So thank you for purchasing this book! Because of you, another book will make its way into the hands of a child who needs it most.

Do you know a school, library, or organization that could use some free books for their kids? We'd love to help! Please fill out the nomination form on our website (see below), and we'll do everything we can to make something happen.

www.bushelandpeckbooks.com/pages/
nominate-a-school-or-organization

If you liked this book, please leave a review online at your favorite retailer. Honest reviews spread the word about Bushel & Peck—and help us make better books, too!

The Adventure Continues!

Join Lucky, Rudy, and Red in more exciting cases with the Good Guys Agency!

Boys for a The Better World
GOOD GUYS AGENCY
Kind Like Fred Rogers
BOOK-FOR-BOOK
Nick Esposito • Ricardo Tokumoto

Boys for a The Better World
GOOD GUYS AGENCY
Brave Like Jackie Robinson
BOOK-FOR-BOOK
Nick Esposito • Ricardo Tokumoto

Boys for a The Better World
GOOD GUYS AGENCY
Sweet Like Milton Hershey
BOOK-FOR-BOOK
Nick Esposito • Ricardo Tokumoto

Better Boys for The a Better World
GOOD GUYS AGENCY
Play On Like Beethoven
BOOK-FOR-BOOK
Nick Esposito • Ricardo Tokumoto

Available wherever books are sold!

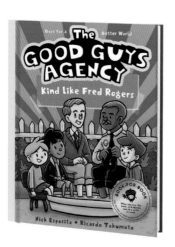